SHEEP FOOTBALL

ALSO BY ERIC PINDER

North to Katahdin
Tying Down the Wind
Life at the Top

SHEEP FOOTBALL
and Other Strange Tales from Rural America

ERIC PINDER

Alpine Books
Berlin, New Hampshire

Illustrations on title page and page 57 by Carol Phenix
Illustration on page 71 by Eric Pinder
Cover photographs by Eric Pinder

Library of Congress Control Number: 2007903134

Part of this book, in abridged form, first appeared in *Bike Culture, Byline, Country Extra,* and *Echoes.*

ISBN 978-0-6151-4526-6

www.ericpinder.com

To Ron and Roberta

In the United States there is more space where nobody is than where anybody is. That is what makes America what it is.

Gertrude Stein, writer

Old fences and old buildings offer no very pleasing views to the possessor, especially if he be in want of means to replace them.

Hiram Harwood, farmer

Literature consists of those books that make a bid for literary immortality, a length of time that Mark Twain defined as 'about thirty to thirty-five years.' I'll settle for that.

Edward Abbey, curmudgeon

CONTENTS

GOING PLACES

ENDINGS

Foreword

CHANCES ARE YOU'LL NEVER read these words.

Worldwide, only about one person in five speaks English. Even fewer *read* English, especially if they have to pay $16.95 for the privilege.

Fewer still bother to read prefaces or author's notes, preferring to skip ahead to the good stuff. "Nothing can be more fatuous than a writer writing about his own writing and the serious reader is advised to skip what follows," says nature writer Edward Abbey in the preface to one of his own books.

If you agree with Abbey, as I do, you've probably already turned the page to chapter one. That assumes you've picked up this book in the first place. The odds were against your doing so. Only three out of ten people in the United States have set foot in a bookstore in the last five years. According to the most pessimistic statistics, more than half of all high school graduates will never read another book for the rest of their lives. Enough people still read books to keep Barnes & Noble afloat, but thanks to television, the internet, and the hectic pace of the twenty-first century, they often have less money to buy books and less time to read them.

With 120,000 new titles published in the U.S. each year, how likely is it that a reader will choose to buy this particular book? An author facing such odds is better off writing a mystery or thriller. Celebrity autobiographies tend to do well, as do practical works such as cookbooks and self-help titles. Books that combine fiction with nonfiction and even (gasp!) poetry, such as this one, fit no specific marketing niche and thus rarely find their way onto the shelves at your local bookstore.

What is this book? It's a collection of stories, essays and a few poems, all with a rural setting or theme. Some are funny, some are sad. Most have been previously published in magazines and journals. The title essay, "Sheep Football," originally appeared in *Country Extra* and was later reprinted several times, earning the author (at the time a recent college graduate) the amazing sum of several hundred dollars. Almost enough to pay the rent! Even more incredible and unexpected was the paycheck I received for the short story "A Morning for Artists and Preachers."

"Are we talking big bucks?" a friend asked.

"Well, no," I replied. "We're talking…lunch." Still, any paycheck at all is a coup in a business where rejection slips are the norm. (See Chapter 5.)

A successful fiction book sells at least 5,000 copies. A successful nonfiction book sells 7,500 copies. Successful poetry books don't exist.

How well will this book do, with its mishmash of genres? Time will tell.

I hope you enjoy these tales from rural America. If you don't, well, that's what amazon.com reviews are for. Or perhaps this book will get no reviews at all, in which case the question of whether anyone is reading these words will have been answered.

[*Clears throat, taps microphone.*] Is this thing on?

SHEEP FOOTBALL

Signs of the Times

IMAGINE MY SURPRISE WHEN I pushed the playback button on my home answering machine and heard a familiar voice: "Hello, this is George W. Bush…"

Beep. That was the only message. Oddly, the President forgot to leave a number where I could call him back.

The President's pre-recorded message told me to get out and vote—and, oh, and if it wasn't too much trouble, would I mind voting for the Republican candidate for governor?

Half an hour later I received five other calls urging me to vote Democratic instead. Even James Earl Jones rang me up that night, though he was just trying to get me to switch my phone service to Verizon. With all the politicians trying to reach me, I'm surprised he was able to get through.

That's the joy of living in New Hampshire, if you're a political junkie. Three years out of four, New Hampshire is just another one of those small, rectangular, unimportant states east of New York. But every fourth year Washington, D.C. moves into town and starts fawning over you. Politicians of all stripes shower you with praise, promise to lower your taxes, pave your roads, finance your schools, and, if you'll permit, kiss your babies. Suddenly you can't turn around without bumping into someone who's running for president. The only escape is to stay indoors and disconnect your phone.

Come January 2004, with a first-in-the-nation presidential primary at stake, I knew my phone would soon be ringing off the hook. I wasn't disappointed.

The phone bombardment started about two weeks before the primary. Most of the calls were from Joe. Senator Joe Lieberman, I mean. But he called to chat so often, I feel comfortable calling him Joe.

The polls weren't in Joe's favor, but a local family-owned two-screen movie theater took down its *Now Playing* and *Coming Attraction* signs and put up a big GO JOE GO, VOTE JOE LIEBERMAN sign. So that's at least one family's vote he was sure to get. I doubted that he would get many more, mainly because most people thought he had registered for the wrong party's primary.

Lacking money for slick TV ads, he was forced to spread his message to New Hampshire Democrats and Independents by hitting the phones. I hope he had a good long-distance calling plan. Half the time the phone rang that week, I'd glance at the caller ID screen and see JOE LIEBERMAN spelled out.

I suppose all politicians are, to a certain extent, actors on a stage. Joe Lieberman, alas, was "phoning in" his performance.

He needn't have bothered. According to the polls, the only contenders with a real shot at winning New Hampshire were John Kerry, Howard Dean, John Edwards, and Wesley Clark. Their voices sore from campaigning in Iowa, they arrived in New Hampshire warning of doom and disaster unless George Bush could be defeated in November. A joke making the rounds referred to them as "the four hoarse men of the apocalypse."

One week before the primary, the up-and-down swing of the official polls was interesting—if dizzying—to follow. I decided to conduct my own, private, unscientific poll. I started counting the number of posted campaign signs springing up in my neighbor's yards.

If the winner had been determined by who had the most signs, then John Edwards might actually have taken New Hampshire and perhaps propelled himself to a national face-off with George Bush. The morning before the vote, someone stuck at least 300 Edwards signs in the snow banks along the roads in my town, and they all were still up when the polls opened.

I suppose those signs didn't reflect the candidate's true level of support, since one dedicated person supplied with an arsenal of signs and a reliable vehicle could have put them all up in just a few hours. But the signs popping up in residential front yards did count. Dean and Kerry were neck-and-neck, with Clark "four-star" signs not far behind.

There's a strange fascination with watching these small, colorful rectangular signs spring up out of the January snow like dandelions in the newly thawed grass of May. A Kerry sign here, a Clark sign there, and, oh look, there's even an odd LaRouche sign.

Looking for campaign signs is, I image, much like the hobby of bird watching. One afternoon I spotted my first rare and elusive Kucinich sign. Then I saw the yellow-throated "Firefighters for Kerry" sign, also rare, mingling with the more common "Kerry blue."

The next morning I discovered and logged three whole species of Dean sign: the common yellow-on-blue Dean, whose habitat ranged from private yards to roadside snow banks; the extremely rare blue-on-yellow Dean; and finally the hybrid "Hope Not Fear" Dean.

On this latter sign, the word "fear" was printed directly above Dean's name. That was a bad design. Competing campaign signs often were clustered together, so portions of the signs were

5

obscured. When the left side of this particular species of Dean sign was blocked, what a passerby first saw was "Fear Dean."

Fortunately for the Dean campaign, this species of sign only migrated into New Hampshire in the last few days before the primary, and didn't find many niches left to occupy.

A week before the primary, the once common Gephardt, much like the passenger pigeon, was thought extinct. Then I spotted a single Gephardt while driving through the tiny village of Cascade Flats. Since only one survived, the Gephardt signs could not reproduce, and probably went extinct the next time the snowplow went by.

Before I knew it, the primary was over. Almost all the signs vanished. Like migrating birds, they flew south for the winter— south to South Carolina, the next big primary on the election calendar. They won't be back for another four years.

New Hampshire sure seems quiet now. My phone hardly rings. I wonder what my buddy Joe is up to these days. For some reason, he never calls anymore.

Ice

The aging process has you firmly in its grasp if you never get the urge to throw a snowball.

Doug Larson, maybe

NO ONE FORESEES THE COMING of glaciers. No one wakens to the sight of four fresh inches of snow on a Monday morning and thinks, "This is the one, the storm that lasts a thousand lifetimes." There's only one way to know a glacier is coming, and that's to see the wall of ice, to guess where it will go, and to get out of the way.

On December nights in Millinocket, Maine, tree branches slick with ice wrap around the streetlamps. The trees resemble glass sculptures, pure and light, intricate and brittle. Electric light pulses through them, then disperses into the darkness. They are like Christmas ornaments planted in the town park.

It has yet to snow. Leftover November leaves, dry and cracked, rustle in the brown grass or twist in funnels around the tree trunks, made buoyant by the breeze. A branch, heavy with ice, sags to eye level. In summer, free from the burden of snow and ice, it springs many feet higher, a safe perch for birds and squirrels. Tonight its branches hold still in the wind. The rod of a streetlamp rises through them, burning yellow at the top. The tree sits inside its cold glass case like an exhibit of summer. A few leaves stick to its top, hard and heavy. The rough, grooved bark is smoothed over.

When snow finally does fall, paths blur and fade; the pothole-ridden road to Roaring Brook fills and vanishes. A boot makes a crisp, heavy footprint in the first inch of snow, but soon withers and fades away. Younger snow fills it in, leaving in time the palest outline of a foot, then only a small depression, then nothing but a fresh white plain, all signs of human passage erased.

The three-pronged tracks of rabbits dash and dart under the trees, hours after the animals themselves have gone. To discover the habits of rabbits in the morning, follow the tracks.

A footprint, while it lasts, dents the whiteness, as if some entity of its maker still hovers in that place. As new snow falls and deepens, filling the cavity, it does no good to renew the footprint. That print, too, soon will vanish. Snow is only patience and water. It outlasts the most dedicated shovel wielder, but yields at last to spring.

But some winters refuse to yield. There were times—many times during the ice ages of the past three million years—when the snow renewed itself faster than it could be melted by the sun. The relatively recent Wisconsin glaciation pushed the Laurentide Ice Cap over much of North America, covering its greatest expanse 18,000 years ago. Today the ice age is waning; perhaps it's over. But what if it's not? What if the ice of this year's winter were to harden on our roads, to stick there despite all efforts of salt and plough, strengthened by snows that fall and keep falling? Suppose that glossy tree on a street corner stays icy into spring? The clear ice swells and darkens until only a dim, distorted shadow of tree is visible. Sleet clings to the streetlamp, thickening. It emits an ebbing trickle of light.

In the woods, bears stumble out of their dens, sleepy and hungry, and flee south in search of food. Instinct triggers a thought in the brains of birds, a need to fly north out of the heat of Florida. The program of migration is hardwired, and they follow its instructions back to higher latitudes, only to find a landscape still white with ice. Warily they circle overhead, confused. Instinct has gone wrong; cold reason sends them away, back to warmer climes.

Snow piles on the streets of towns, burying them more and more as April edges into May. The weather becomes front page news. The Sunday *New York Times* claims it's the harshest winter on record, a fact that is obvious to everyone. For a week in late May, the sun shines. Some of the snow melts, but not enough. It refreezes as a slick ice layer. In time, the snow level rises. Cars disappear underground. In June, the highway department abandons the roads. A press release explains that ploughs can clear off layers of fresh snow, but cannot attack the thick ice underneath. The National Guard is called in, and the first of what soon becomes a dozen towns is evacuated by helicopter. Civilization retreats south.

Houses appear to sink underground, one floor at a time, as the snow layer rises. Ceilings collapse, and scattered cracks ring like gunshots all around town as mounds of ice bring roofs careening into basements, there to lie buried by snow. The trees fail to sprout new leaves and die. Grasses and shrubs, denied sunlight for a year, also die, never to return. Bright orange jackets freeze in deserted houses invaded by snow. No one from rural counties goes hunting next December; there is nothing to hunt, no one to go hunting with. The roof of a hospital on Somerset Street holds up briefly but the building itself is lost under ice; an antennae protrudes from the whiteness, like a wand of grass in a field. Soon the last roof caves in. The smokestacks at the paper mill in Millinocket expand and crumble, plugged with ice. All traces of the once-bustling downtown district of town are gone. Farther north, the craggy peaks of mountains turn to hard white lumps in a monotonous world of white. The glacier has returned.

Continental glaciers swept repeatedly over North America during the Pleistocene Epoch, two million years ago, when the ancestors of our species stood erect for the first time. These pre-humans were a stunted race by our standards, undernourished yet ill-equipped to hunt food, with cramped brains that spared little room for rational thought. But unlike their cousins, the apes, their brains continued to grow, and straight spines freed their hands from the burden of locomotion. This evolution took place on the warm plains of Africa, long sundered from North America, still rapidly pulling away from the New World across the Atlantic.

The continental glacier sucked water from the northern seas and froze it, dropping worldwide ocean levels a maximum of 400 feet. It thrust a great sheet of ice south over North America. The land that is now Maine, New Hampshire, Vermont, and New York did not escape, but neither did it suffer a slow death, buried gradually under newer and newer snows. It was ploughed down, destroyed, scoured clean by the onslaught of ice. No houses or human dwellings of any sort interrupted the vast coniferous forest, for people did not exist yet. But there were trees—thick forests lost to a long, deadly winter.

Caribou lived in those woods, and savage bears, and strange mammals never seen by human eyes. If they looked north they saw a tongue of ice, hundreds of feet thick, inching closer month by month, snapping the trunks of trees under its weight. In spurts, spurred on by heavy snowfalls on its northern flank in Canada, sections of the ice giant shifted their weight and slid softer layers of ice down over older, harder layers. In the middle of the early-Ice Age forest, in a land that would much later become the village of Millinocket, the view of this approaching monster was blocked by a heavily forested mountain, tall and smooth, much like the Great Smokies of today. It did not yet have a name.

Caribou watched the ice coming, felt an ominous chill in the wind and migrated south. As the ice sheet advanced, mindlessly pursuing them, it struck the mountain, surged briefly upward, but fell back. Instead, year by year, the ice seeped around the sides, crushing the forests to the south but leaving the high peaks untouched—for a time. The advancing bulk of the continental glacier pushed to the coast, plunging into the relatively warm waters of the Atlantic.

Smaller valley glaciers already had formed on the slopes of the mountains. Frost pried loose boulders and crumbled each mountain's wall. Ice began to carve out the basins called cirques. The continental glacier swelled; the level of ice rose through the millennia, creeping up the side of the mountain and onto the alpine tablelands, and then at last to the highest peaks. The summits, and the entire edge of the North American continent, sagged under the weight of mile-high hard ice.

Every hundred thousand years or so, the sun pushed back the ice, warming the exposed rocks. Soil accumulated on bedrock. Plants began to bloom. The shade of trees returned, birds sang in the branches, and animals much like squirrels jumped from tree to tree. Somewhere, thousands of miles distant, a half-human cut open its thumb on a jagged chip of slate and moments later invented the knife. But soon the sun again turned a cold shoulder to the Earth, and ice crept down from the Poles.

SNOW, WATER, ICE, AND WIND are the four elements of winter. Three of these entities share the same ingredients yet scarcely resemble each other. They shape the land in different ways: Ice does the digging and splitting, water transports soils and clays, snow insulates rocks and trees against the fierce winds. Wind, the fourth element, sculpts ice, swirls snow into great mounds, and stirs the still water on the surface of ponds. Wind carries warmth and wind carries cold; it directs where the ice will go. Ice age winds push Arctic air masses deep into the south to nullify the warmth of the sun. Ice sheets bury a continent; a hundred thousand years later wind breathes warm air on the glaciers, sending them scurrying back to the poles.

Snow has eased off in recent years. I've missed it. Once it was possible to hope for a white Thanksgiving and not be disappointed; a white Christmas was guaranteed. Now these events are not so certain. May surprises, such as a foot of sticky snow, are all but unheard of. The Earth has warmed, is warming still, and the memories of glaciers fade off in the distance like the ice cap over Greenland.

The average surface temperature of planet Earth is currently 59 degrees Fahrenheit, or 15 degrees Celsius, thanks in large part to the natural "greenhouse" effect—the emitting of heat by so-called greenhouse gasses in the atmosphere, such as carbon dioxide and water vapor. Without it, the average temperature would plummet to nearly zero degrees Fahrenheit—a permanent, planetary deep freeze.

The increasing number of newspaper headlines about global warming reflect fears that the greenhouse effect may someday run amuck, boosted by a human-induced increase in carbon dioxide, heating the globe to intolerable levels. But the Earth's climate has swung from hot to cold many times in the past. In the middle of the last glacial epoch, the average global temperature sank to only

49 degrees Fahrenheit, 10 degrees lower than today. That's all it takes to trigger an Ice Age.

Climatologists have estimated that temperatures during interglacial warming periods are sometimes five or more degrees *higher* on average than today.

Slight variations in the tilt of Earth's axis, a 93,000-year fluctuation in the eccentricity of the planet's orbit around the sun, and the fact that Earth spins like a wobbly top around its axis on a 25,000-year cycle all play a role in modifying the climate over long stretches of time. Who knows what the future may bring?

Last year, for months, there was nothing to indicate that winter had arrived—just dead grass leaning over a thin dusting of snow. It was February before the hills looked like proper winter, before the trees stood hunched under shoulders of white.

Inside my grandmother's house in Millinocket it's artificially warm; the air hums with the sound of heat pumped through pipes. Outside the window the sky is black, but a fat bush scrapes against the frosted glass, and on it rests a fresh white coat. It's 4 A.M. I go out to walk in the first real snowfall of the year.

There's a moon somewhere in the fog, but it can't be seen. Up close the air is clear. I can see the slope of the ground, see the limbs of spruce trees holding up blankets of snow four inches thick. It's too dark to see the snowflakes still falling, but I can feel them drift across my face, land on my shoulders, and slide down the fabric of my coat. The sound tells me the precipitation is a dry snow, needlelike and small.

Close by, the gurgle of creek waters is strong and clear; in daylight this sound would hardly be noticed. The air is alive with a soft light that comes from everywhere and nowhere. A bright yellow glow ignites suddenly on a hilltop. I hear the pounding of a car's motor—an old car, struggling and coughing. The sound draws nearer, and headlights shine across the ground. It's a sudden, blinding explosion of light. For a moment, the air is filled with a billion floating snowflakes, each one twisting and spinning in the wind. Then the car goes past and all is dark again. Snow falls, quiet and invisible.

A Purr-fect Storm

You've probably seen or heard of Inga and Nin, the famous Mount Washington Observatory cats. Meet Jasper, the shy, seldom-seen tabby cat who lived with them both on the windy summit of New England's highest peak.

I FIRST MET JASPER THE CAT on a chilly evening when westerly winds were whipping across the summit at seventy miles per hour. I stood alone on the mountaintop and watched a dark fist of cloud punch slowly toward the peaks, beaching itself on the rocks. Gray mist slpashed on the boulders like ocean spray. As I stumbled through the fog, bullets of hail nipped at my face, and the hood of my jacket flapped like a sail. With each strong gust, the precipitation can I was carrying squirmed in my arms like an angry cat.

I encountered a truly angry cat back in the shelter of the observatory. Jasper was not a happy animal when I rudely walked in from the cold and picked him up; I even had the nerve to try to pet him. He squirmed and struggled in my arms until I let him go, but graciously accepted a bowl of milk as a peace offering. He even begged pitifully for a second peace offering two minutes later.

15

"Is Jasper an outdoor cat?" I wondered aloud.

One of the meteorologists laughed. "I wouldn't say that. The only door Jasper waits in front of is the refrigerator's."

For fourteen years, Jasper has survived inside the warm belly of the Mount Washington Observatory while sleet and hail battered the windowpanes and hurricane-force winds rattled the walls. Outside, sheets of ice rain have shattered on the rocks like glass, but a snoozing Jasper has purred through it all.

Like most cats, Jasper is a hunter. One night, he trotted off into the twilight and jogged back with a mouse tucked between his jaws. He deposited his prize in the doorway and ran back for more. By night's end, a row of rodents lay scattered across the observation deck, sorted by size. Everyone was surprised.

"He was stacking them up like cordwood," announced one early riser. We expected the Environmental Protection Agency to show up any minute to declare the American house mouse an endangered species.

What's so odd about an orange tabby cat who lives on a mountain and likes to eat asparagus? In Jasper's case, quite a bit. He often flees in terror from children but tolerates adults, so long as they hold him upside down (he hates being held right-side up) and put plenty of milk in his drinking bowl.

For more than a decade, a traumatized Jasper played second fiddle to Inga, the famous calico cat with frosty whiskers. Inga was always the teacher's pet, the spoiled child. A darling of the media, she was "interviewed" by *Cat Fancy* magazine while a jealous Jasper sulked in obscurity.

A picture of an icy Inga is still printed on T-shirts, posters, postcards, and refrigerator magnets that are sold each summer in the Mount Washington Museum gift shop. When Inga passed away in 1993 at age nineteen, her estate generously donated all proceeds from her modeling career to the Observatory.

Sadly, Jasper has enjoyed no such notoriety. While thousands of Inga postcards are shipped to mailboxes all across the continent, poor Jasper lurks in the shadows, far from the public eye. Even worse, a new nemesis named Nin appeared on the scene in 1996, just when Jasper finally thought he had the summit to himself. (Rumors to the contrary, Nin's name is not short for nincompoop—though it should be!) Nin poses for the cameras and purrs in the arms of visiting journalists. He also robs Jasper's food bowl when the older cat isn't looking.

Jasper, patient as always, endures. The only legacy of this big, shy, but basically friendly cat is likely to be a clump of orange furballs left behind on the living room rug.

Excerpted from Life at the Top: Tales, Truths & Trusted Recipes from the Mount Washington Observatory.

Reflections

Beads of dew glisten
on the chlorophyll-green shaft
of a single stem of grass.

In the stillness of each small pond
burns a tiny yellow sun.

Schrödinger's Rejection Slip

I USED TO THINK THAT science and the business of writing had little in common. Then one day, while shuffling a stack of bills, junk mail, and returned manuscripts, I had a flash of inspiration: If science could eradicate small pox and other diseases, why not rejection slips as well?

A quick study of physics revealed that I was onto something. In theory, I could rid the world of rejection slips in a matter of minutes. Weary postal carriers would rejoice. Writers and scientists everywhere would hail my discovery.

My patented technique for rejection-slip removal owed much to Erwin Schrödinger (1887-1961), a man who dabbled in the quirks of quarks and other strange things. Like Einstein (a "relatively" good scientist), Schrödinger helped publicize the peculiarities of modern (or quantum) physics.

What is quantum physics? Simply explained, quantum physics is really weird. For example, imagine that a kitten and a tube of poison gas are placed inside a box. A 50-50 chance exists that the tube's lid will open spontaneously. If so, then the gas is released, killing the kitten. But you can't see inside; the box is sealed. What has happened? Is the cat dead or alive?

Actually, the cat is neither—in fact, it isn't even in the box! So bizarre is Schrödinger's universe, the cat isn't "real" until a conscious mind becomes aware of it.

The implications for writers are staggering. If a kitten in a box isn't real, neither is a rejection slip in an envelope.

Yesterday I received a letter from the offices of a well-known consumer magazine. The editors there had liked my work in the past, often scribbling notes of praise in the margins of their off-white rejection slips. But they never bought my stories. Common sense told me to expect another rejection.

I fought off disappointment by applying the "Schrödinger's Cat" technique. No way could that envelope contain a rejection slip—unless I was foolish enough to open it. Deep inside that #10 SASE boiled an ocean of quantum possibilities, a world of shadows, ghosts, and uncertainties. Until I peeked inside, nothing else existed.

In the end, of course, I succumbed. The envelope beckoned to me from the edge of my desk, tempting me hour after hour.

"Hmm," I said to myself, "this envelope looks awfully thick." I held it up to the light, squinting. Row upon row of ink blackened the envelope's translucent skin. "Surely," I thought, "that's too much writing for a rejection. It must be a contract!"

I tore open the seal. Immediately, the murky quantum sea stiffened and congealed. A single sheet of paper surfaced amid the waves.

Biting my lip, I read the first line: "Dear *Contributor*..."

The cat was dead. Long live the cat. Q.E.D.

Peeking Behind the Page

I CONFESS, WRITERS LIE. Here is an example.

Three pennies and a crumpled receipt from Dairy Mart grow warm on my palm. I toss them all at a corner of my desk, then stride past to stuff a bag full of milk, yogurt, and orange juice into the refrigerator.

Behind me, the coins smack wood. One hits edgewise, rolling toward the wall, and lands with a metallic clatter on the radiator. Silently, the receipt glides and settles over the remaining pennies.

So far, all this is true. But wait.

The receipt from Dairy Mart curls up vertically, and on this little paper tent squats a black bug. When did it land there?

I don't spot the bug until an hour later, as I prepare to leave for town. I snatch my wallet off the desk, sit in the chair to tie my boots.

The bug doesn't move.

Curious, I loom over it, squinting down at its furry little body. Nothing happens. Hundreds upon hundreds of compound eyes gaze back, unblinking. Four wings perch on the insect's back, poised for flight.

Soon I must leave; hours pass. By the time I come back, a red sun is already melting on the western hills. The shadows of oak trees sprawl across the tall grass as if crawling east to escape the night.

In all this time, the bug hasn't moved. Not one millimeter. Is it dead?

A night passes. The sun rises in the east, and the shadows of trees now slink west toward the mountains. The bug is still there. It hasn't stirred, hasn't shifted so much as a single, stick-like leg. Whatever waxy glue insects use to walk on walls seems to have cemented this one's feet to the paper.

Surely, I think, the thing is dead. The bug landed on my grocery receipt...and died. An omen, perhaps? I'd better check the expiration date on that milk.

As a test, I reach down and shake the receipt, certain that a dead husk of insect will float to the floor.

Instead, the bug leaps at me, buzzing angrily. It twists in mid-air and darts behind the curtains.

End of story.

Is the story true? Yes, in parts. A bug really did perch on that slip of paper for twenty hours. But the receipt could easily have come from Price Chopper or a bookstore or the post office. I've forgotten. Or perhaps I know exactly where it came from and am only feigning uncertainty.

Writers do this; we twist the truth. Our work is easier this way. We must poke and prod each sentence with the sharp points of our pencils, furiously beating down the prose till it behaves. And the words fight back tooth and nail, like caged tigers gnawing at the bars. Too often the words break free and are lost forever. Other times, they submit at last, chained to the paper by loops of black ink.

After such an ordeal, the writer who has tamed a sentence is reluctant to let it go. A drastic error, a fatal flaw sometimes makes this necessary. Only little white lies get passed over, considered harmless. It's easier to change the truth than the prose.

What if there were no pennies from Dairy Mart? What if I kept in my pockets just a set of keys and a quarter, rather than three copper portraits of Lincoln?

My groceries that day cost $5.78. I handed over six dollars and three cents, to avoid the unwanted two pennies in change. "The only thing pennies are good for are avoiding more pennies," I said.

The short, bespectacled woman behind the counter laughed and nodded vigorously. She handed me a quarter. "That's about it," she agreed.

Or did she? Does it matter how much the groceries cost? Am I at fault if a woman with perfect vision appears suddenly in glasses? A literalist might accuse me of blinding her. I disagree. Even so-called creative nonfiction is just fiction to a lesser degree.

In her essay, "Living Like Weasels," the writer Annie Dillard walks to a pond near Tinker Creek and, for an instant, trades her soul for that of an animal. She and a weasel lock eyes; an exchange of bodies occurs.

I doubt the weasel saw it that way, however. He was probably just startled or annoyed. Even Dillard may have considered the encounter mundane. A writer of nature doesn't burrow down in a weasel's soul and then, a full week later, struggle to recall the details. No, she would have sprinted home and scrawled a rough draft on an envelope, a cardboard box, anything.

I think she started with a sentence, a simple idea: "A weasel is wild, who knows what he thinks?" Nine words and a glimpse of weasel, that's all.

Not much of a story. But to exchange souls with a weasel— now, *that* is an idea.

"I tell you I've been in that weasel's brain for sixty seconds, and he was in mine," she claims. Perhaps. I suspect, though, that most of her sixty seconds of weaselness came sitting at a desk, pen in hand, and lasted for hours. She *did* inhabit that animal's brain, but not on any path in the woods.

Much later, as the sun sank below the hills, as shadows deepened and disappeared in starlight, as the weasel retreated to his lair—somewhere, miles away, a writer behind a desk started to probe its soul.

Occasionally the truth and the prose coincide. This all leads to another small story, another black bug. I meant only to brush away the bug from the corner of my notebook, where it had landed. It started crawling in the way of words, its tiny brain too stupid and preprogrammed to worry about impeding the literary process. I hovered over it like the sky, unseen by insect eyes.

With a fingertip, I tried to nudge it into flight. Instead, I killed it. The bug's fragile, invertebrate body smudged like an ink stain, a streak of black across the clean white paper. A smear of life, gone in an instant.

It gave me something to write about.

Honest.

These words stain the empty page.

Black tracks of ink—
Footsteps through the snow of a blank white world.

Regarding Mr. Sanders

AT THE LAST MOMENT HIS hand shot out and snagged a metal girder. Paul steadied himself but did not pull back to safety. Not yet. Gazing down at the brown water, Paul imagined the river rushing up at him. All he had to do was let go. So easy.

Ripples and wavelets glinted below. A flake of rust or paint fell loose off the bridge and floated ever so slowly downward into water. Paul estimated the distance at thirty feet. He squinted. How fast would *he* be going when he struck? How long would it take to die? That would make an interesting calculation for his students at Middlebury High School. Perhaps, if his courage failed this morning, he could put the question on a quiz.

Paul knew that his weight, about 150 pounds, was irrelevant. He would fall at the same rate no matter what he weighed; Galileo had proved that in the seventeenth century, supposedly by dropping cannon balls off the Tower of Pisa, timing their descent with his pulse. The balls, no matter their shape or weight, always fell at the same speed. Paul's students should know that by now. He had told them Galileo's story often enough. Weight mattered only for a light object such as a feather, or a flake of rust, slowed by air resistance.

Paul glanced at his bony hands and his coat sleeves, hanging loosely on his arms. He was turning into a scarecrow. But the lost weight didn't matter. If he jumped now, he would accelerate down toward the water at the same rate as one of Galileo's apocryphal cannonballs: 9.8 meters per second per second—another statistic Paul's students should know by heart. He would impact the water in just under a second, traveling about 21 miles per hour.

Not fast enough. He needed to think of a better solution to his troubles, or else find a taller bridge.

Abruptly, he yanked himself back to firmer ground and turned away. He brushed the rust flakes off his sleeve and walked off the footbridge into the town park. A dirt path led the way. The gurgle of river water receded behind him.

The air was cold that late autumn morning, the thirteenth of November, Paul's birthday. He watched the water vapor in his breath condense in the chill air. A tiny cloud slipped through his lips and floated, then quickly disappeared. Strange, he thought. He had spent most of his adult life teaching physics to children, and yet the beauty of science—the condensation of clouds, for instance—had always eluded him as a child. His foster parents had fed him the Bible, but little else. They had tried to mold Paul, like clay, in their own image. He had rebelled, moved away. Even now, years after his foster parents' deaths, they were the reason he was standing in this park and no other, his new shoes moist with soil and wet leaves. He came here to think, when he had time.

The Middlebury Town Park was an island of grass wedged between Granite Road and North Grand Street, and Paul Sanders stood at its center. There was no place to sit so he leaned against an oak tree, breathing deeply. The brisk walk had tired him.

He turned to face the sidewalks and the stream of cars. It was a short walk through the park. There was no playground or bike path, just an arched footbridge over the river, an aesthetic construction for sightseers driving by on North Grand. Autumn

27

had fallen on the park. Patches of red, yellow, and brown leaves dried and faded on the ground. As Paul walked, he observed the shapes and colors and identified the species of each leaf.

His foot came down on something hard—a wallet. Paul had thought the wallet was just one more brown leaf until he had stepped on it. It felt fat and heavy. He stuffed it into a coat pocket.

There was a man asleep in the tall weeds on the side of Granite Road, and Paul thought the wallet might belong to him. He called out to the man, and instantly regretted his decision. Drunks don't carry fine leather wallets. The man would lie and take the money for liquor.

The man's eyes opened when Paul spoke. They were empty eyes, the color of alcohol. Paul looked away, feeling foolish. A path circled the park; he followed it to get away.

The pulse of cars in the street switched on and off as the lights changed from green to red. The sound of a droning engine rose in pitch as it hurtled closer, then lowered and faded as the car shot past, like a sudden expired breath. Paul knew the phenomenon well. Forty-six years of teaching physics had trained him to listen for red shift and blue shift on the streets of Middlebury.

Paul was afraid the drunk might follow him, so he took the crosswalk to put a barrier of cars between them. A red car drove by fast and something small was thrown out a back window—a cup, filled with brown liquid. It landed at Paul's feet and rolled forward. The liquid trickled down through cracks in the cement. Paul couldn't see who had thrown it; faces in the window were blurs of motion. They had shouted something but the word was inaudible, stretched and distorted by the Doppler effect—a classic example. Paul knew they had thrown the cup at him deliberately, but he shrugged off the attack. The thrown cup was just a brief act of spite, harmless and temporary. The physics stayed the same.

The wallet was still in his pocket, half-forgotten. He thumbed through it now, expecting nothing but a few bills and credit cards. A glance, however, revealed a sum of several thousand dollars. The bills were crisp, each no more and no less than a hundred dollars. There was no identification: no license, no credit cards, no family pictures, just a loose slip of paper with a name and address. William Thompson, Cedar Village Road, 34B. The handwriting was in large block print, childlike. But a child did not carry two thousand dollars in large bills.

The wallet sat in his hand, weighted like lead. A police car drove by, as if on cue. Paul watched the wheels spin slowly, too slow to dissolve into a blur. Paul stuffed the wallet back in a coat pocket and walked briskly away. A street corner was no place to pilfer another man's wallet. The time was still early morning, and except for the breakfast cafes, shop windows were barred. Paul didn't want to be seen loitering in front of a closed store, not with this wallet in his hand.

Cars filled the streets but the sidewalks were empty. People had just begun to drive to work, their days full and expectant. Paul envied them. Since his retirement he worked only as a substitute, and the principal's office at the new high school seldom called him. He had been put out to pasture. But he, too, had a job today. He had decided. He would return the wallet to its owner.

A Santa Claus stood in front of the bank at the corner of South and Main, ringing a small bell without enthusiasm, the way a lazy wind rings church bells. Paul stopped to catch his breath; the man looked at him impatiently, frowning underneath a fake beard. He was young, and the white beard apparently itched. He pulled it down every few seconds to scratch at his chin.

Paul waited till he was rested. The Santa Claus twitched an arm to ring the bell, then turned and took a sip of coffee from the cup on the table behind him. Nothing was said about Merry

Christmas; it was too early for that. Above the man's cup, rising steam condensed in the cold air. Paul saw the swirls and eddies of the wind traced in the motion of the steam. Next to him the walk sign sputtered to life and the flow of cars thickened and stopped. He tossed a coin in the collection jar—it felt like a quarter—and crossed the street.

Two phone booths were in the alcove inside the drugstore on Elm Street. Both were occupied, one by a swarthy man, the other by a young woman chattering in Spanish. When the man left, Paul stepped in and closed the door to shut out her voice. He opened the wallet and slowly counted nineteen 100-dollar bills, then rifled through the folds hoping for anything, a business card or a scrap of paper. A single nickel fell out and rattled on the tin floor. Nineteen hundred dollars and five cents.

"Hey mister!"

A set of knuckles struck the glass in front of Paul's face. A man crouched outside, pounding against the phone booth wall. Paul looked down at the man's dirty white sneakers and cheap raincoat. The man hadn't shaved, his face a field of black stubble.

"Use the phone or get the hell out of there!"

The Spanish woman kept talking. Paul had turned his back to her but could sense her watching. He stared the other man full in the eyes and willed himself not to blink. One hand held the wallet; with the other he picked up the receiver and tucked it under his chin. There was no need to dial; the man backed away, his mouth open slightly, eyes dull.

The woman fired an angry monologue into the other phone. Her small, dark eyes were reflected in the glass. Paul could see her staring; he didn't blame her. Why would a strange man run into a phone booth, pick up the phone but not dial?

Nothing else was in the wallet, just the address of William

Thompson and nineteen hundred dollars. Paul left the nickel on the floor. He pushed open the door and stepped out, eager to get away from the woman. She had strange eyes, stern and dark like a bird of prey. Paul stepped away quickly.

He had to wait at a crosswalk for a change in the lights; this time, he wasn't alone. Shops had opened and a stream of people coursed along the narrow walkway between storefront windows and a row of parked cars. Middlebury could no longer claim to be country. The town had become a city, enlarged by two decades of immigration and industrial progress.

A second Santa Claus appeared, this one more enthusiastic. He had gathered an audience of small children and their parents, telling stories about the North Pole. A sharp wind whipped around the corner of the building, reddening the man's cheeks. It made him look authentic.

Santa Claus called to Paul. "Happy holidays, sir! We're building a playground for the kids at Mayfield and sure would appreciate your support."

Paul reached in his coat pocket for some spare change. His hand came up empty. Embarrassed, he walked away. Santa Claus threw words at his back. "Merry Christmas anyway, sir!"

Paul stopped, and an eddy formed in the stream of people on the sidewalk. Santa's bell fell silent. "I've already given," said Paul. He had dropped a five-dollar bill in a red Salvation Army pot just yesterday. And he had done so much more. How could he explain?

A brief silence fell, then Santa's bell clattered once more. The stories of the North Pole continued. Children laughed. Someone tossed in a handful of coins. Paul heard them rattle on the bottom of the collection jar behind him.

He almost turned back to give away the wallet. That would build them their playground and save him a trip to Cedar Village.

Instead, he walked on.

The cement ground was hard and Paul felt it jar his knees with every step. He took smaller strides and tried not to look down, afraid to catch himself in an act of superstition—avoiding the cracks.

Paul fingered the wallet. He had nineteen hundred dollars in his hands, nearly half as much as he had earned teaching in 1959, his first year at Middlebury High School. That same year he had worked as a janitor on weekends, for extra cash. Now he was old and alone; nineteen hundred dollars would provide a nice life for weeks. The money had simply come to him, like a gift. It was waiting on the ground in the park, waiting to be found by someone who deserved it. But somehow just taking the money didn't seem right. Paul wanted, even needed, to find William Thompson, if only to learn what sort of person had so much and discarded it so carelessly, while he himself had only a meager biweekly check in the mailbox.

The bus to Cedar Village left every hour on the half-hour. The route went past Paul's old school, now in the slums. The highway had been moved to the other side of town, taking with it the stores, the banks, the schools. Forty-six years of Paul's life was boxed into that old school building, forty-six years of textbooks and coffee breaks and labs. Now it was derelict, waiting to be knocked down and replaced by low-income housing.

Cedar Village, however, had begun to see new life recently. The old middle school was there, where he used to teach piano on Thursday afternoons. The building was a library now. The town had built a playground behind it, two years before his retirement, when he had served as principal. He had given some money to the project, back when he had had money to give. The playground design had been his. They had named it after him.

The bus rattled along Main Street. Paul shut his eyes but couldn't get comfortable in the hard plastic seats. He squirmed like a child and sensed the pity and scorn of the other passengers. Every cough or cleared throat was a disguise for laughter. But no one stared. They looked straight ahead, stone-faced. When Paul looked at them they dodged his eyes, pretended not to notice.

The bus pulled into the curb and a crowd flooded out the back. There was a clicking sound up front where people dropped coins in the machine next to the driver. Paul's stop was next, Cedar Village.

For a short stretch on Maplewood Drive, the storefront windows were black and empty. He used to walk here from across town, back when a body could still get a sandwich and a cold drink at the Deli. Back when it was safe. Back when he could manage the three-mile walk without gasping for breath.

Now the old supermarket was boarded up. Broken glass littered the parking lot. They sold drugs inside—marijuana, cocaine. That's what his students had said, years ago. God only knew what went on in there now. The memory brought to mind Mr. Thompson's wallet: almost two thousand dollars and the handwriting of a child. Was he taking a small fortune to a boy? An illiterate, a criminal? Why did Paul, retired after a respectable career, find more in the dirt of the town park than he found in his own mailbox? He was no longer certain the money belonged to William Thompson.

Behind the old supermarket was the former site of Middlebury High School. Too small to support the population of an expanding city, it now stood vacant and soulless, waiting for the wrecking ball. Paul stared at the building and felt wistful. The inside of the bus was dirty, so Paul licked a finger and wiped a small, clear circle through the dust on the window. Through it he watched houses and their little square lawns slide by, one by one.

Outside, the tires kicked up a layer of mud and covered the peephole.

"Excuse me." A hand brushed against his shoulder. Paul stiffened but tried not to flinch. It was just a harmless old lady in the next seat back.

"Excuse me, but does this bus stop at Cedar Village?"

The answer was obvious, printed on a sign at the front of the bus. If she had bothered to notice when boarding, she would not have needed to ask. Paul almost didn't answer—but what did it matter? "Yes, of course," he said.

"Thank you."

Paul looked through the muddy glass and saw a new village rising out of the ruins of the slums. Boarded-up windows and broken glass were being replaced by a line of small white houses, all the same. Assembly-line architecture for those who couldn't afford the finer homes across town, or for leftover old folk from back when the place was respectable. The old lady might have been one of these.

"You're welcome," he said, far too late. The woman started.

At Cedar Village, Paul and the remaining passengers emptied out the back while a new group began to fill the front. Paul stayed at the curb and watched the bus drive away. The wallet weighted in his pocket, but he was in no hurry to get rid of it.

A construction crew was in the process of widening the road. Orange flags stopped the bus at the end of the street, and workers scurried around its sides. The air was filled with a metallic clamor, the sound of a jackhammer breaking open the road.

A row of maple trees shaded the street, but each tree was stripped of leaves, letting through small blocks of sunlight. Paul walked along and heard the hubbub of children playing soccer in someone's lawn. A soccer ball shot out from underneath a parked car and rolled to a stop at his feet. Two children ran out after the ball, a boy and a girl who might have been brother and sister. Their voices faltered when they saw Paul.

He smiled, or tried to. He meant to just tap the ball with his foot, to send it back to the children, but his kick went askew and sent the ball at an angle down the center of the street. Paul tried to apologize but the children didn't wait; they chased after the ball. Paul erased his smile.

The remains of the Middle School stood up ahead. Behind the school was the playground, the one they had named for him, partly for his years of community service, partly for his five-hundred-dollar check. The playground was full today, but not with children. A wrecking ball and a crane peaked above the rusty swings, and a swarm of construction workers in orange jackets worked at its base. This was where the bus had stopped and Paul now saw why. They were turning his playground into a shopping mall.

The change was logical. No one went to school here anymore. They were bussed across town. Did it matter? Paul no longer cared. He couldn't afford to.

Cedar Village Apartments consisted of three buildings arranged in a circle just off the main road. Apartment 34B was dead center, upstairs. No one was in the lobby, but Paul could hear a child crying nearby. Somewhere above him lived William Thompson.

The stairwell was filthy. Someone had tracked mud up to the second floor. Two sets of footprints were crisply defined in the mud; Paul followed them up. At the top of the stairs he heard a new sound join the baby's cries—an argument. There were two voices, one male, one female. They shouted at one another, at first alternately, then joining in a crescendo with a third voice, also male.

The argument came from 34B; the crying baby was somewhere

else down the hall. Paul stood outside the door, his hand half-raised to knock. A glass or plate crashed against the door and shattered. He listened to broken fragments settle on the floor like so many tiny bells. The door had trembled with the blow. For a moment he feared it would swing open, reveal him, a stranger, where he should not be, with money he should not have.

The door stayed closed. Behind it the shouting reached a climax, then fell into silence. Inside a door slammed, then another and another. Paul felt the air grow tense, cold. A gust blew through the grate at the end of the hall, and pages of old newspaper rolled across the floor like tumbleweed.

There was a muffled cry, a thud, then silence.

Paul stepped back. The hand he had extended fell limply to his side. Go in? Knock down the door? Run? He felt his pulse quicken. On the other side of the door he heard the approach of footsteps—heavy booted footsteps.

Paul turned his back on the home of William Thompson and hurried to the stairs, then down toward the street. He held the wallet tightly in his hand. The hard soles of his shoes clacked against the steps with militant regularity, like a message tapped in Morse code. The noises echoed up the stairwell. Behind him, harsh and abrupt, a door opened and then slammed shut in answer.

The Universe in My Backyard

THE WORLD WE KNOW VANISHES once the sun goes down. Shadows deepen. Vistas fade. The stars ignite. Suddenly we are forced to rely more on our ears than our eyes.

Tonight the sky is silent and clear, but the woods are dark, impenetrable, and noisy. Behind me I can hear the footsteps of some unseen creature snap and crunch twigs, then stop without explanation. What is out there? I quicken my pace.

I am walking home alone down a rural road in western Massachusetts. To my left lies a farmer's hay field. I cannot see it, but I know it is there. In daylight I would be able to see four rows of wooden fence posts joined at right angles, barricading the field inside a tight rectangular box. In that box grows an acre of clover, alfalfa, and wild grasses. Green reeds sway in the wind. Tens of millions of grasshoppers, ants, and assorted insects scurry in the dim, green-tinted world beneath the tall grass.

Just this afternoon I stood here watching a bumblebee buzz and glide inside that field, searching for nectar. I stood outside the fence, looking in. At my feet, the knee-high grasses abruptly ended. No flowers poked through the soil to attract the attention of the wandering bee. The wind found nothing to rustle or stir. I was alone, beyond the boundary of the fence post and tiny universe it contained.

Now I have returned. I rub my hand over the knobs and grain of the rough wooden fence; the peeling paint is no longer visible, but I catch a sharp, painful flake in my palm.

The barrier between the tall alfalfa and the tight-clipped grass at my feet still exists, although the boundary now is more difficult to see. I can scarcely detect the two separate worlds, one wrapped around the other. The world of the hay field is boxed in, enclosed. The world beyond, where I stand, seems endless.

A thousand bright sparks ignite all at once in a corner of my eye, distracting me from my thoughts. I turn to look. It is the flicker of fireflies. Their soft lights shift and churn like a galaxy dying and then reborn. Inside and directly above the field, they form a rotating, fast-paced replica of the Milky Way.

Strangely, the fireflies fill only the air above the field. Not a single flicker emerges beyond the rectangular confines. The outer universe where I stand stays dark. The fence post upon which I lean my arm is a barrier that no fireflies cross. I wonder. Why do they limit themselves to that small region of open sky, as if encased in glass?

The answer comes to me a moment later. Of course, I think. The flies and crickets (also the bats and larger creatures that prey upon them) stay where they are because the universe immediately beyond the fence line holds no tall grasses, and therefore no food, no mates. Their little universe inside the fence contains all they need.

For another hour I observe the shifting constellations of fireflies. Not a single stray spark shoots into the unexplored abyss behind the fence where I watch and wait.

One night I woke to see a dim flash in the upper corner of my bedroom window. I peeked out from under a roof of sleepy eyelids. The source of the light, I supposed, was the high beam of a car angled so that the light penetrated the glass. But soon another flash came, and another. Drugged with sleep, I mumbled, "Busy traffic tonight. Wonder why."

A full minute passed. That was how long it took for a series of electrical impulses to jump from synapse to synapse across my brain until a coherent thought emerged. I knew something was wrong, but could not quite piece the puzzle together. I lifted a hand to wipe the crusty sleep from my eyes.

Over and over the light flashed, yellow and weak. Finally, the appropriate synapse in my brain came to life. The solution to this new mystery jolted me fully awake. *Smack.*

I wasn't facing the window.

I was rolled onto my left side, my arm tingling from lack of circulation. From that position, I should have been able to see nothing but a solid black wall.

My eyes popped fully open then, just in time to see another impossible flash of color illuminate the windowless wall. A glowworm had somehow penetrated the room. In a zigzag pattern it streaked across the dark air, shooting out photons from its luminous posterior. For a time the insect hovered over a bookcase, then it flew from corner to corner as if searching for a way outside. Occasionally it swirled in loops as if caught up in a miniature tornado. I heard a faint, angry buzz.

Tonight I cannot sleep. I sit up in bed, watching yet another firefly flicker in a corner of the room. Where do these explorers come from?

For half an hour the insect flashes on and off near the ceiling lamp's glass enclosure. Even when the insect finally moves out of view, I can hear its body thump against the glass. It is trying to get away.

Suddenly the firefly changes tactics. A streak of yellow light shoots toward me like a meteor, headed straight for my eyes. I blink and yank up an arm to fend off the attack; the firefly pulls away.

Now the insect clings to the wall, hidden behind a heating pipe. Its light escapes around the edges, casting a yellowish stain on the wallpaper. For an hour it sends out regular strobes like a pulsar. It is a solitary star in a lonely sky.

What does that firefly think, limited as it is by a miniscule, instinct-driven brain? Does it think at all? Is it aware of its entrapment inside this room, cut off from the rest of its species? The firefly perches against the wall, boxed in. Helpless. Somehow it has stumbled into a starless alien universe; it has slipped into a black hole from which there is no escape—unless by chance it finds a crack in the window screen, a wormhole to the larger universe outside.

The firefly's pale glow is the only source of light in this room, the only voice in the dark. Its intermittent flashes are a desperate plea, a way of saying, "Here I am, here I am. Where are you?"

No one answers, no one sees—except me, of course, and I do not count. I almost feel sorry for the creature. I am too large, too unfathomable. I do not exist in the firefly's perceptions except as a blur.

The cosmos of my bedroom into which the firefly has accidentally wandered is small enough to let me stand flatfooted on the floor and brush my fingertips across the ceiling. The walls are slightly farther; I must walk three steps to reach the horizontal barrier of this universe—three footsteps to the edge of eternity.

At this moment I could play God. I could shout, "Let there be light!" With a flick of a switch on the wall, I could drown the firefly's glow in a brilliant, fiery incandescence such as it has never before experienced. To overwhelm the firefly, all I need is a 60-

watt bulb from General Electric. The lightbulb holds a latent power; it is a furious dark star waiting to go supernova. All that's required is the touch of my hand.

But I hold back. The glowworm flickers again. The rate of its flashing has slowed. Perhaps it is getting tired. Perhaps it is dying, ever so far from home.

The efforts of that firefly make me wonder. What lies beyond the fence posts of our own fourteen-billion-year-old universe, past the glow of quasars on the cosmic horizon at the beginning of time?

For most of human history, the invisible barrier of our own atmosphere kept us firmly in our place. Until 1957, the only flights beyond the confines of the Earth's mesosphere were flights of the imagination, piloted and powered by the explosive intellects of a handful of geniuses and dreamers. Cyrano de Bergerac first suggested the exploration of new worlds via a fictional rocket ship in the 1650s. Decades earlier, in an era when speculative fables about outer space were rare in literature, Johannes Kepler wrote one of the first science fiction novels about a voyage to the moon. The very title he used, *Somnium*, suggested how impossible the act seemed.

Kepler wrote his dreamy epic during the same era in which he and his contemporaries were refining the details of mathematics and physics—Kepler's own Laws of Planetary Motion among them—that would one day make his vision a reality. But that day would not come for another 300 years. There were too many obstacles.

Too far, too difficult, why go there scoffed the naysayers. Centuries passed and technology improved only slowly. The geocentric Ptolemaic universe was comfortable and cozy, so why stir up trouble? Such was the common wisdom. Humanity was satisfied with what it had.

The weight of hundreds of miles of air pressed down on people's shoulders, while gravity snagged at their heels and pulled them both physically and metaphorically back to Earth. Eventually, the ambitions of any would-be spacefarers always landed with a thud.

At the dawn of the twentieth century, Robert Goddard and his liquid-fueled rockets were laughed at and mocked in the popular press. His missiles never reached as high as the upper stratosphere, and perhaps that was just as well. Friends and enemies alike insisted that his rockets could not travel in a vacuum, anyway; the boosters would have nothing to push against outside of Earth's atmosphere. Thus, space was forever sealed. In the minds of many, the wings of the Wright brothers were fantastic enough. The public did not need or want any other miracles.

Goddard's greatest achievement, perhaps, was not the launching of rockets, but simply casting light on the problems and potentials of space flight. He aimed for an unknown region beyond the fence posts where no one else had ever thought to go. As his rockets flared, people heard the roar and turned their heads to look. Some of them never looked back.

In the science of ballistics, in order to break free of Earth's gravity well—to launch a ship into space and visit the moon and beyond—requires a thrust of 6.98 miles per second. Anything less, and a rocket either goes into orbit or else plunges back to the surface. To visualize why this occurs, simply grab a pebble or baseball and hurl it into the sky. For a few breathless moments the object will rise up from the surface against the force of gravity. But gravity wins in the end. The rising baseball slows, momentarily hovers at apogee, and then accelerates quickly downward toward the center of the Earth. If you hurry, you might catch it before it lands.

To throw a baseball that never comes back requires an incredible speed attainable only with a powerful rocket: almost seven miles per second. To break free of the *sun's* massive gravity and leave the solar system, starting from the Earth, requires an even stronger push, 26.4 miles per second, more than 95,000 mph. Only three human-made spacecraft have done so, and they are now heading toward the distant stars.

Of course, rockets *do* function in the vacuum of space. Newton's third law of motion, the conservation of momentum, states that "for every action there is an equal and opposite reaction." A rocket thrusts gases out one end and propels itself in the opposite direction. Goddard's critics were wrong.

Nonetheless, not until 1957 did human beings take that first, tentative step into a new, larger universe. *Sputnik 1* looped around the planet at a maximum altitude of 598 miles, beeping ominously (to the Americans) and triumphantly (to the Russians); it sparked a competitive space race between the two nations. After two months in orbit, it burned up in the atmosphere.

In November of that same year, *Sputnik 2* carried the first live animal—an unfortunate dog named Laika who did not return alive—to the brink of space. Next, *Luna 1* became the first craft to escape the pull of the Earth's gravity. A human named Yuri Gagarin first entered the fringe of space in a metal husk called *Vostok 1* in 1961; unlike the dog, he splashed into the ocean and returned home safely. Other astronauts and cosmonauts followed, and a handful actually stamped their footprints in the silvery dust of the moon, starting with Neil Armstrong and *Apollo 11* in 1969.

The moon was just another fence post, and in the years that followed, human beings peered more and more intently into the strange environment outside our own tiny, enclosed field. In the 1960s and 1970s, Russian and American crafts landed on the surfaces of Mars and Venus. The *Voyager* spacecraft flew toward the outer plants and sent vividly detailed pictures—images that Galileo with his weak refractor telescope would have died for—back to Earth. The last image from *Voyager*, after its flyby of Neptune and the icy moon Triton in 1989, depicted the Earth as a pale dot in a starry field, far, far away. The data from which that picture was compiled crossed the cold expanse of space for six long hours at the speed of light before reaching the Earth.

In time, *Voyager* may cross beyond the heliopause, the faraway limit where our sun's solar wind merges with interstellar space. *Voyager* is one of a few curious fireflies we have sent toward the stars.

Physically, only a handful of human beings have ever been so far as the moon, a mere 240,000 miles away. A few more, put into orbit by rockets and the space shuttle, have gazed down at the curvature of the Earth from an altitude of little more than a hundred miles. The rest of us are still boxed in, our eyes looking up instead of down.

The space shuttle did not launch until 1981, and the maximum height to which it reaches barely qualifies as space. A desperately thin outer layer of the atmosphere called the thermosphere still swirls around the shuttle even at its absolute ceiling, about 300 miles. Though we occasionally launch robotic probes to faraway worlds, we are otherwise like curious fireflies who perch atop the fence post and gaze at the strange universe beyond, but dare not fly across the line—yet.

Nonetheless, our visions and dreams have hurtled outward farther than ever before. The COBE spacecraft (Cosmic Background Explorer, launched in 1989) and other radio telescopes probe the distant galaxies and can detect the faint aura of cosmic microwave background radiation, an "echo" of the Big Bang. At the other extreme, computer models depict in vivid color the death throes of the Milky Way hundreds of billions of years from now, when the oldest stars will exhaust their fuel and a black hole will hungrily feed on the last remaining wisps of light. Theories predict the continued expansion of the universe, with galaxies beyond the Milky Way becoming distant and faint.

I've always been fascinated by the concept of an expanding universe, with not just solid matter flying farther and farther apart, but also space itself growing in size. The Big Bang was not simply a knot of matter exploding outward into a vast empty space that already existed. Instead, space itself hurtled outward; the walls of our metaphorical room grew in size, and are growing still.

If there is an ultimate limit, a boundary formed by three dimensions plus time, then what sort of meta-universe exists beyond it? I remember when the firefly was pressing against my wall, trying to escape—is that what it would be like to come at last to the end, to discover that there is no more to explore?

We may never know. Fascinating though it is to imagine someday touching a "wall" at the extreme edge of the universe, that is not how nature works. There is no edge. Physicists believe our universe is bounded infinite, endless in three dimensions—but not necessarily in four. Just as the two-dimensional surface of a desktop globe seemingly goes on forever—trace your finger along the equator and you will never come to an end—still the sphere is curved and bounded in three dimensions. We can see this closed curvature directly in a way that a hypothetical two-dimensional creature living on its surface cannot. Likewise, it is the curvature of our own three-dimensional cosmos that challenges the imagination. At the limits of our universe exists a "boundary" difficult to visualize—and impossible to touch. But does this mean it is also impossible to cross?

The Earth's atmosphere was once such a boundary, a wall too large and too high to breach. The very first hot air balloon was invented in 1782 by two brothers from France, the Montgolfiers. Maximum heights of four miles were achieved by 1804. Balloons that reached twenty miles arrived in the 1920s. That was the extent of our exploration into "space." That was humanity's first probing of the inner fence line.

Visually, of course, it was possible to travel much farther. As far back as 1609, Galileo's primitive telescope magnified the craters and mountains on the surface of the moon and detected the four inner moons of Jupiter: Io, Europa, Ganymede, and Callisto. He gazed out beyond the fence line and wrote about what he saw. Others soon followed his example. But not everyone was pleased.

Some were fearful of what they might find. One of the clergymen sent to investigate Galileo's preposterous claims refused to look through the telescope; he was "sure" that no moons of Jupiter existed, and would not be fooled by the trickery of any newfangled device.

Space was too far away, and not everyone wanted to go there, in thought or in deed. Even the story of the Tower of Babel in the Bible issued a clear warning against reaching too high or too far. In the land of Shinar they built a tower into space, but God disapproved and destroyed their efforts, for fear that "henceforward nothing they have a mind to do will be beyond their reach."

The Church authorities placed the old scientist, Galileo, under house arrest. His visions of a tiny Earth that moved around the sun discomforted them; they preferred the old view. But according to rumor, when Galileo recanted under threat of torture and officially denied the Earth's movement through the heavens, he mumbled under his breath, "Nonetheless, it does move."

Galileo's parting jab may be apocryphal; no one knows for certain. What we do know today with scientific precision is the size of the Earth and its elliptical movement relative to the sun, an average of 93 million miles (150 million kilometers) away. We can track the orbits of our neighbors in space, from the swift gyrations of Mercury, closest to the sun's heat, to cold and distant Pluto, more than 3.6 billion miles away. We know approximately where we sit in the larger universe beyond the sun's influence—in the Orion arm of the second largest galaxy in the Local Group. We orbit just one of trillions of stars. We have emerged from our tiny enclosed field into a universe much larger and more fantastic than anyone ever expected. A long, long time will pass before we press up against another wall, helpless like that firefly in my bedroom, and suddenly find we can go no farther.

The *Voyager 1* spacecraft is one firefly that flew beyond the fence posts, carrying with it a number of souvenirs from Earth. *Voyager* now travels through the silence of space alone. Whoever—or whatever—encounters the spacecraft on its long journey will find recordings of whale songs, samples of fifty-nine human languages, and a sound-and-image collage of nature on Earth.

The two *Voyager* spacecraft, like the *Pioneer* mission to Jupiter that preceded them, have launched toward the distant stars and will move through the Milky Way for millions of years. They are not the only signals we have sent to the stars; our radio and television transmissions leak into space at the speed of light. We have at long last gone over the edge of the fence posts and are now calling out to any that can hear. Our probes and transmissions are a message to the silent, lonely cosmos, our way of saying, "Here I am, here I am. Where are you?"

Sheep Football

A GUST OF WINTER WIND rattled the windows, lights flickered, and icicles plummeted off the roof, landing in brittle, glassy chunks on the porch floor. It was dawn, time to feed the sheep. I shivered and stepped outside.

"How are you this morning?" I asked the sheep, stripping twine off a bale of hay.

"Not baaa-ad!" they replied.

There were about forty of them, all huddled together under a maple tree like bushels of white wool. The tree's spidery black branches leaned over them protectively, trapping the thin warmth that rose from their bodies.

I quickly tossed some alfalfa into their feeder, but that wasn't enough to satisfy the sheep. They wanted pelleted feed—lots of it—and told me so, bleating loudly.

While I scooped feed into a bucket, the sheep staggered to their feet and lined up, ready to tackle me. The game was about to begin.

A twenty-pound pail of pellets was my football, and the bulging white eyes of sheep stared at it greedily. As soon as I stepped over the fence, the animals swarmed around me, trying to knock me down to get to the bucket in my hand.

Feeding them had become like a game of football. I had to dance and dodge, looking for a hole to run through the flock. A co-worker of mine once called sheep "the stupidest of mammals," and now I knew why. All the feed-troughs were buried beneath their bellies. They were standing in their own feeders, begging for breakfast. Where was I supposed to pour the feed?

Gradually I waded through the logjam of sheep-backs. I fought my way toward open ground, deep in the middle of the field. The sheep bleated in protest. I squeezed to the front of the flock and jogged ahead a step or two, holding the bucket far in front of me—a play-action feint.

The sheep, of course, fell for the ruse and chased the bucket. And while the flow of sheep streamed ahead of me, I spun on my heels and sprinted back across the snow to the now-unguarded feed troughs. Could I reach them in time?

Like a running back loose on an open field, I tucked the grain bucket under my arm and barreled forward. Forty linebackers gave chase, baaaing pitifully.

Closer, closer, almost there...I lowered the bucket, ready to pour out all the feed in the split second before the sheep arrived. I was just a step away from a touchdown...

But they caught me at the last second. Two big lambs ran past me to the right and left, then abruptly turned in below my knees. The rest of the flock pushed from behind; I felt their fleece, wet with melting snow, rubbing against my jeans.

My body spun, hurled against the fence. It felt like being struck by a sledgehammer. At impact, the bucket slipped free from my fingers. It hit the ground and exploded, spraying a million tiny kernels of grain across the ground. Gleefully, the sheep gathered round to celebrate the fumble by munching on brown pellets off a tablecloth of white snow.

At least they stopped bleating; it was quiet again. I stood and rubbed my aching shoulder, then limped to the sideline like an injured athlete.

Minutes later, I staggered into the farmhouse, where my friends were still working. "I've been to hell," I announced. "It's full of sheep." Everyone laughed at me.

Despite my sour mood, I had to laugh—I had been outplayed by the stupidest of the mammals. It was a humiliating experience.

The next morning, grim and determined, I tried a new ploy. I brought along a teammate with brains—a border collie. Together, we won the game.

Looking Up

I WAS TEN YEARS OLD and lost in space. I wanted to be an astronomer or, better yet, an astronaut. Carl Sagan's *Cosmos* series on PBS captivated me; unfortunately, a few years later, college-level calculus did not. I could do the math but couldn't *feel* it intuitively, and for a successful career in astronomy that's not good enough. My soaring hopes of traveling the universe landed with a thud.

Still, I kept looking at the sky. Even with the cheap, four-inch telescope I'd bought as a teenager it was possible to gaze across trillions of miles and millions of years back in time. The rings of Saturn showed up as a tiny, glimmering disk, reflecting light that took hours to cross the solar system and arrive at Earth. It chilled and thrilled me even more to realize that light from the Andromeda galaxy had just ended a two-million-year journey by bouncing off my telescope's mirror into my eye.

One thing I noticed right away was that stars shimmered, while the planets shone with a steady, unbroken light. Why?

The answer, I learned, had more to do with Earth's own atmosphere than with interstellar space. The starlight we see on a clear night passes through turbulent sections of the sky that have different temperatures and densities, and at each boundary the light refracts or "bends." As a result, the stars flicker.

All stars (save the Sun) are so far away that they look like mere pinpoints, much like solitary pixels on a black computer screen. But a planet is close enough to appear as a disk, composed of multiple pixels. Each individual "pixel" on that disk is refracted and bent as it passes through our atmosphere, but the disturbances more or less cancel each other out. Therefore the planet's light shines steadily. Planets don't flicker because they're closer, and therefore look wider, than the point-like flames of the stars.

Some nights, of course, no stars are visible at all. Clouds—or, as frustrated stargazers call them, "that stuff"—block the view. So one day I focused my attention on "that stuff," and discovered it was just as interesting and intriguing as the stars.

Today, I like to think of meteorology as "local" astronomy. Looking at clouds on Earth isn't so different from observing dust devils on Mars or the swirling, red-hued clouds and storms of Jupiter. The only distinction is that the planet we're studying is also the planet we happen to live on.

My interest in both weather and astronomy stayed with me through college and beyond, but it was weather that became my career. Astronomy, though, was my passion.

For years now I've worked at a meteorological observatory on the summit of New Hampshire's Mount Washington. The alpine weather's fascinating, but the mountain also provides a terrific platform for watching the stars, planets, and the Milky Way— when it isn't obscured by fog. With little light pollution and a thinner atmosphere overhead, the stars sparkle. Sometimes observers on the summit can see curtains of white or green from the northern lights, where charged particles pouring out of the nearest star—our Sun—collide with our upper atmosphere and ionize it. As one book poetically puts it, the aurora is where "the sun's atmosphere touches our own."

I'm supposed to be watching the weather, but the summit crew and I like to walk onto the observation deck whenever the wind calms and the stars glimmer. Some nights we're even able to watch the path of the space shuttle or the International Space Station overhead. Other nights we see meteors—shooting stars—chunks of glowing meteoric rock heated by friction as they enter Earth's atmosphere.

Meteors look pretty, but they don't have anything to do with weather. If you've ever wondered why the study of weather is called "meteorology," while the study of actual meteors is called "astronomy," blame Aristotle. His book *Meteorologica* described everything that fell from the sky, which he called "meteors." Technically, meteors include rain, snow, and hail—not just tumbling pebbles from outer space. (More specifically, rain and snow are considered hydrometeors.)

Aristotle was undoubtedly brilliant, but he was off the mark about a few things. Comets he believed to be atmospheric phenomenon, a strange sort of cirrus cloud high in the sky. He never realized how "high" those comets actually were.

This afternoon on Mount Washington neither comets nor clouds are visible in the sky. As I write these words, high pressure is building into the region, drying up the clouds, promising a fine view of the stars all night. Here on the summit we're enjoying terrific 95-mile visibility with scarcely any wind. Hard to believe that just a few hours ago the wind was gusting to 86 mph and we could hardly see the ends of our noses. Now the sun is setting and the sky is darkening. If all holds to form, the visibility won't be just 95 miles tonight—it will be infinite.

The Poet Behind the Telescope

JOHN MILTON WROTE HIS EPIC poem *Paradise Lost* at the close of a century and a half of scientific discovery—an era in which Copernicus, Brahe, Kepler, and Galileo collaborated on their own version of "Astronomy Found."

Galileo's innovative use of the telescope revealed new wonders in the heavens. Craters on the moon, the phases of Venus, and the satellites of Jupiter all helped awaken astronomers and philosophers from the two-thousand-year slumber imposed on them by Aristotle and Ptolemy.

Milton himself was fascinated by new discoveries. But even though Milton once visited the elderly Galileo and probably gazed through "the Glass," as he called the telescope, the poet had little interest in the science behind the scenery. The geologic properties of the moon, the parallax of stars, the formulae to determine the elliptical orbit of planets—none of these matters would have concerned him. Instead Milton admired the universe as a great work of art, not as a machine whose wheels and cogs moved in set patterns to be analyzed by human beings. According to Milton's poetry, the study of the heavens was either fruitless ("too high to know what passes there") or pretentious ("be lowly wise: Think only what concerns thee and thy being.")

In *Paradise Lost*, the angel Raphael censures Adam, telling him that the secrets of God should not be "scann'd by them who ought/Rather admire." Still, even though Adam's curiosity is frowned upon, it isn't prohibited outright. (Galileo probably wished the Church of his day had been so lenient.) Raphael clearly considers the pursuit of knowledge a misguided but understandable attempt to better learn the glory of his Creator:

To ask of search, I blame thee not, for Heav'n
Is as the Book of God before thee set,
Wherin to read his wond'rous Works.

Milton did honor Galileo and his telescope—but only for revealing the beauty of the cosmos, not for the support they gave to Copernicanism and the upstart heliocentric theory. Galileo was, to Milton, "the Tuscan *Artist*," not the Tuscan *astronomer*.

Milton's appreciation of the telescope was solely for its ability to show the grandeur of the Greater Artist's work, much of which was hidden from the naked eye. Milton's poem pointedly makes mention of the beauty of the phases of Venus (one of Galileo's key discoveries) and of the "Pleiades dancing." Milton considered the telescope a simple device to be used "as when by night the Glass/Of Galileo, less assured, observes Imagined Lands and Regions of the Moon."

In the then-raging debate between geocentric and heliocentric models of the universe, Milton was a neutral party. This allowed him to appreciate the telescope as something other than just a weapon of Copernicanism. The telescope showed him "Spaces incomprehensible" and multiple worlds, and it did not matter to him that these discoveries appeared to refute the astronomical teachings of Ptolemy and the Church.

Milton counts as a Copernican ally only insofar as he rejected the well-ordered and fully explained Aristotelian model of the universe, which had dominated Western science for centuries. He conceded that the universe did contain mysteries unexplained by Ptolemy and Aristotle. Far from disturbing him, those mysteries actually pleased him—after all, the complexity of the universe made it not only possible but certain that human efforts to understand it sometimes would be in error—including, perhaps, the heretical Copernican system. "Earthly sight, If it must presume, might err in things too high."

In Milton's day, Ptolemy's system was still widely taught, Copernicus' original system was being modified and improved upon by Kepler and Galileo, and the scientific community had only recently rejected "compromise" theories such as Tycho Brahe's. Brahe, the man without a nose, proposed a model by which all planets except Earth revolved around the sun, while the sun—with planets in tow—then orbited the Earth. It was enough to make one dizzy.

In the light of such controversy, educated non-scientists such as Milton may have concluded that all theories were in some ways incorrect or incomplete. A scientific model such as Copernicanism was viewed as a metaphor for the truth—nothing more than a convenient mathematical device for predicting the motions of the planets and keeping the calendar accurate. In *Paradise Lost*, the angel Raphael states exactly that opinion when he says that epicycles—Ptolemy's attempt to explain the apparent retrograde motion of the outer planets—are "to save appearances." In Milton's eyes, Copernicus may have invented a slightly better way of tracking the planets and making sure Easter landed on the right day, but that did not make his model "truth."

The deeply religious Milton turned the dispute between the Church and Science into an amusement for God, a farce to invoke "His laughter at their quaint Opinions wide." Milton's own opinion was the same as the angel Raphael's. He did not care whether it was the Earth or the Sun at the "Centre of the World." All that mattered was that the beauty of the universe could be appreciated as art—which is probably why Milton became a poet and not an astronomer.

An Eye for Detail

THE BLACK BEAR REFUSED TO accept relocation, returning three times to the Windy End Campground, where the food was better. He was a friendly bear, as bears go, and tourists thought it was great fun to watch him steal bacon and granola bars from the sacks of food they tied to trees outside their tents.

"Have you seen the bear?" they always asked new arrivals at the campground. Two people had the luck to capture the bear on film, and an instant photo of the beast facing the camera, one paw deep in a food sack, circulated from tent to tent. It was generally agreed upon that the bear looked guilty. They even gave him a name, "Barley."

Park authorities were less amused. What if the bear ransacked a tent? What if, startled by a flashbulb, it mauled one of the campers? So on Monday, Phil Surman started his workday by driving Barley to Taylor's Ridge to be shot.

Ben Tucker, an older ranger, pulled the trigger. Phil never touched the gun. But he watched the killing and later helped bury the carcass. An hour after the execution he sat behind his desk at base camp, idly tapping his badge on a panel of oak. In his left hand, clenched into a fist, a pencil point protruded like a yellow thorn. He welcomed the day's first tourists with a grim smile.

PHIL'S FIRST DUTY THE FOLLOWING Friday morning was to give directions to Thomas Peterson, a tall, blond photographer from Boston whose mouth twisted into a quirky smile when he spoke. Peterson announced that he meant to hike to Minnow's Pond, down a narrow, little-known trail in the valley, where there was no clear view of the summit.

Phil, in the meantime, was obliged to stay inside the rangers' cabin. A glass of murky spring water and a radio were his only company, though Benjamin, his boss, promised to come at 10 A.M. to help with the influx of weekend campers. For much of the afternoon they would lecture tourists who didn't know what to do with their trash, or who wanted to know where the restrooms were found.

Phil and the other rangers had seen Peterson often over the past three weeks. He hiked to a different campsite every few days, taking pictures along the way. Usually he came back to the base camp to register his new position, which is what brought him to Phil's desk that morning.

Quickly, the photographer scribbled his name and destination in the book; Phil leaned over, checking to make sure it was legible. When Peterson was almost out the door, he stopped to adjust the small daypack he had borrowed from his friend Joe Forst, another ranger. "I hear the bear was seen again Monday," he asked Phil.

"Yes, up near the Slide. But you probably won't see him at Minnow's Pond." Phil poured a glass of water. He lifted it to his lips, then reconsidered and offered it to Peterson. The photographer couldn't ask awkward questions if he were drinking.

Peterson refused the glass with a wave of his hand. "You have to capture him if he stays around the campsites, don't you? So no one gets hurt?"

"Yeah, that's state law. We'll be pretty worried if Barley shows up again."

After a quiet moment, Peterson went out the door. At the start of the trail he turned, waved, and entered the woods. Phil returned the wave, too late to be seen.

The conversation troubled Phil. He thought about Monday morning and grimaced at what he had done. Just one hiker—a thin, athletic teenager with a ponytail—had heard the fatal gunshot; she asked about it. Phil fed her a lie about hunters picking off starving deer. It was autumn, after all. That ended the matter, for the moment.

Benjamin had ordered the affair hushed up. He put up a sign in the back room: dead bears mean bad business. A joke, but Phil didn't laugh. He had driven a tranquilized bear to Taylor's Ridge and watched it die. Now his job was to lie to the very people who had given the creature a name. Peterson might be the first person today to ask about Barley, but surely he wouldn't be the last.

Phil had met Peterson, or rather found him, two weeks ago in a fog, during the first week of October. A gray haze dropped from the sky, filling the woods with mist. When Phil left his cabin at 5 A.M. the fog wrapped around him, blinding him, letting through nothing but a glimpse of moist grass on the ground, a small patch that moved with him as he walked. In fog there were no complaints of troublesome bears, no lost tourists to find, nothing but wisps of gray, a soft wind, and birds in the trees. Phil stretched out his arms and watched them turn white and pale, shrouded in the mist. He felt like a ghost, floating above an empty world, free from burden.

Then he heard a distant bothersome whistling. It wasn't wind and it wasn't a bird. Every few minutes the sound repeated, like someone practicing a song. Phil walked closer. A tree limb, dark and heavy, materialized in front of him, hovering there. He plucked a wet leaf from the bough and stepped past. The leaf dropped a cold sprinkle of dew on his hand. Behind him, the black branch vanished.

Phil found the whistler on the edge of a clearing, a half-mile or so off the trail, lost but not worried. It was Peterson. Peterson had come to the woods at dawn, hoping to catch the first rays of sunrise cutting through the last of the fog. No one had been in the rangers' cabin, he explained, so he decided to walk about a bit on his own. He had brought no pack, just a camera and a bottle of water strapped to his waist.

Phil knew where they were. He wasn't worried. Soon the sun would push away the fog and reveal the trail. In the meantime the two men sat on the grass, each with his back against a tree. They were only a few yards apart, yet barely able to see each other. For an hour, Phil spoke with the gray outline of Tom Peterson, a shape that grew more and more distinct as the fog thinned and the talk went on.

Seven o'clock, Friday evening, Phil found himself on the trail to Minnow's Pond, half a day behind Peterson. Few people stayed overnight at Minnow's Pond, he knew. Mostly they followed the river for its waterfalls, cascades that thousands of years ago had carved out a thin, green valley in this corner of New England. Hikers used the trail as a detour around the summit. The few who stayed a while, like Peterson, were treated to a land rich with animal life. Deer drank in the pond and the birches and maples were thick with sparrows, darting from tree to tree. A perfect place for wildlife photographers—there were no people to get in the way.

Phil grumbled and stretched. He had spent much of the day behind a desk at base camp and had emerged only once, to chastise a group of students. He spit angry words through his teeth. They were smoking and drinking at the foot of the trail. Brown bottles were tossed behind a shrub in a heap of broken glass, and cigarette butts smoldered on the dry leaves. Phil stamped out their ashes with a thrust of his foot.

At the time, he had felt an urge to rip open a trash bag and dump it back where it belonged—at the feet of the tourists who had dropped it. Let them walk over broken bottles and candy wrappers; they seemed to want it that way. If Peterson had come out of the woods just then, Phil would have shouted, "Look at this mess! I have to put up with this each day." But no, Peterson was somewhere deep in the forest, hoping to capture the bear, Barley, on film. He was enjoying nature.

Phil snorted and frowned. "Taking pictures," he mumbled. He had no time to play in the outdoors. He had a job to do, and his present trip resulted from one more regulation. Joe Forst, the resident at the campground, had radioed down that the pack of medical supplies was missing. Though the pack wasn't needed immediately, regulations required that it be ready, just in case. "Better not wait till tomorrow, " Ben had told Phil. Phil was looking down at a requisition form on his desk, ignoring the moody red twilight peeking in through the windows. He bit his tongue. To take a pack up to Minnow's Pond was an extra chore, and at this late hour it meant a long sprint up the trail. Ben was too old for such a race; besides, he had seniority and could tell Phil what to do.

Tomorrow, no doubt, they would send Phil back to base camp, give him time to treat his sore shoulders, then back up with a new load. Another worker-bee day, and at its end he must smile bitterly into Peterson's camera and pretend to be happy. Leisure was left for the tourists.

The river started as a trickle at Minnow's Pond, but swelled and deepened as its waters tumbled down toward base camp. It crossed the path at two places, with only a single, soggy plank of wood serving as a bridge. Phil had just crossed the second bridge, which sank under his weight. Phil felt cool river water gush through his boots. With any luck, he thought, he would arrive at camp in the last light of the sun, just in time for Peterson's flashbulb to blind him. Then he would wait in his bunk until morning, when Benjamin handed out the next chore.

The roar of river water could be heard the entire length of the trail. Phil could hear the water slap against the boulders on riverbanks, but he had no time to listen. It was simply background noise as he jogged along the trail. The woods and ferns were no more than a flash of green as Phil raced against the sun, which hung low in the treetops, threatening to drop at any moment and turn the forest dark and impassable. Phil concentrated on each quick step; his heavy boots punished the ground. Squirrels and chipmunks that had posed for Peterson earlier that morning scurried away in panic as Phil approached.

The sun lingered for a time in the tops of the trees, but it sank down into the lower branches when Phil was still two miles from camp. Shadows deepened. The man and the sun would complete their race under a roof of branches that stretched for miles. The only break in the canopy came directly over the trail, where tree limbs thinned to let a little pale light spill into the labyrinth.

Phil looked down, so as not to catch his foot on one of the thick roots jutting across the trail. In the mud between the roots lay a mishmash of human footprints, the tracks of fourteen hikers who had passed this way since morning. Phil had seen them off, each and every one. Seven of them had asked after Barley: where was he, was it safe to feed him? Phil told the truth: he hadn't seen the bear since Monday—no one had. Now his heavy boots sank in the mud, obliterating the footprints of earlier hikers. One of those sets of feet belonged to Peterson.

The straps of the medical pack dug into Phil's shoulders. There hadn't been time to adjust it properly, such was his need to beat the sun to Minnow's Pond.

A bright flicker of sunlight cut through the birch trees. Then it was gone. The sky went deep blue. The sun was near the horizon, where the sky dropped down on the edge of Vermont. Phil hurried. There was no moon tonight, so if he lost his race with the sun he would have to crawl at a snail's pace, shining his small flashlight on the bark of every tree to see the blaze of blue paint that marked the trail. The light might hold for a half-hour, but no more. The blue in the sky was draining away, leaving a thick purple. If Phil reached the campground it would be seconds before sunset, a photo finish. And Peterson would be there to take it.

A root wrapped around Phil's ankle, pulling him down. The ground was soft mud. He stood and threw a handful of dirt at the trees.

This was wrong, he thought, hiking the same trail day after day, tripping over roots in the dark. He envied Joe Forst, who called Minnow's Pond his home. Forst sat inside his cabin on rainy days and played chess with stranded hikers. Joe liked to listen to birds and could identify them by their calls. When campers brought children, Joe whistled with the birds to amuse them. Phil, too, used to work with kids at a petting zoo in the Catskills. Now, ruefully, he was paid to execute bears. Poor Barley.

The sun slipped lower. Minnow's Pond was close, but Phil now had to squint to see; only the ground at his feet was clear. He found Peterson's path at last, a set of deep prints off to the side. The tracks led to a hemlock and a bush with a patch of blue and white berries. The photographer must have knelt there for a picture. Peterson's tracks weaved in and out of the worn path. He had a long, leisurely stride.

Twigs and dry leaves cracked under Phil's weight. He quickened his pace for the final sprint. If he didn't trip on a root or sprain an ankle, he was sure he could reach Minnow's Pond before dark.

The race ended suddenly, unexpectedly. The roots and dirt of the trail lifted in the shape of a large moose. The animal's dark hide merged with the shadows and Phil, intent only on the ground before him, nearly walked into the enormous creature. The moose napped in a lingering patch of sunlight that fell warmly on its back. It lay across the trail like a wall. The sheer bulk of the creature awed Phil, as did its nearness, just a yard or two away. He had been so lost in thought, so blind, he had nearly kicked the animal, frightened it away.

The noise made by Phil's boots warned the moose. Its head was raised, alert. Giant, inhuman eyes stared back into Phil's own. The moose watched him carefully for a moment but saw no danger. Even lying down, it was tremendous in size, and had only to rise to tower over the man. Phil stayed still, calm, respectful. The moose settled back to its nap, cautious but unafraid.

Phil's first thought was that this scene belonged to Peterson's camera. But he shook his head, dismissing the idea. The moose could not be owned, its size reduced to a snapshot. The moose would leave with the sun—too late for Phil, but he found he didn't care. He couldn't climb over the animal. There was no easy detour. Low branches and shrubs formed a web alongside the trail; he could fight his way through but the trees would fight back, vines wrapping around his arms and thorns tearing at the skin. He refused to stumble into camp tired and bleeding, all for the sake of a half-minute's light.

Phil regretted only that nightfall would soon drive the moose away. He sat, content to watch while the sun allowed it.

THE RACE WAS OVER, the sun burning a victorious, brilliant red in the leaves. Gradually the last light drained from the sky and filled the woods with blackness. Distant rows of trees vanished in the dusk as if erased. Soon Phil was alone.

He sat a long while after the moose had gone. The other rangers would come for him if he did not arrive soon. Let them. For now, he was content to listen to the wind, to hear the soft patter of misty rain falling on the leaves. A flicker of starlight poked through the trees, and he watched a red pinpoint—the planet Mars—swing across the sky until it was eclipsed by branches.

Phil rose slowly, reluctant to return to the business at hand. His flashlight cut a white hole in the night, bright enough to keep to the trail. He breathed in a lungful of cold air, then set one cautious foot ahead of the other.

An hour later he walked into camp. A strong light spilled out the door of the rangers' cabin. A few candles shone in the woods, near the lean-tos. A murmur of conversation drifted up from the pond.

It was ten o'clock. Phil strode up to the cabin and rested his back against the wall. A flashbulb exploded in his face; it was Peterson, lying in wait. "Hello, Tom," said Phil.

Peterson and Joe Forst, the ranger who had called down for the pack of supplies, were both on the stairs when Phil's vision returned.

"You're a bit late," said Peterson. "Two hours late. What did you do, lose yourself along the way?"

Phil slid the pack off his shoulders. "Yes," he said, smiling. "I did."

Bear with Me

ONCE I SAW A BEAR riding my bike.

I know, that's an old joke, the kind of gag Groucho Marx would've thought up if he'd ever competed in the Tour de France. "How the bear got on my bike, I'll never know." For me, though, the bear was no laughing matter.

It was a sunny July day. Inspired by Lance Armstrong's uphill battles in the Pyrenees, I searched for a steep, challenging hill. I finally found one in a sleepy town in New Hampshire. It was my own personal Alpe d'Huez.

"This is impossible," I told myself, gazing up. It was crazy to think anyone could ride a bicycle up that wall. Heck, if the road were any steeper, I'd need ropes and pitons instead of pedals.

The hilltop protruded into a low cloud. I shifted down and started the ascent.

"You must have the strongest legs in the world, buddy!" a man on the sidewalk shouted.

"I'm working on it!" I called back.

A paved road lined with houses led toward the top. Halfway up, a boy about seven years old saw me, blinked in astonishment, and hollered to a friend somewhere behind his house: "Biker! Someone's riding up the hill!"

"No way!"

The first kid shouted again, impatiently, "Look! Look!"

Apparently no one had ever ridden a bicycle up that particular hill before. I was the afternoon's entertainment.

Huff, puff. My legs burned; my lungs ached. Lance Armstrong and his legacy, I decided, had nothing to fear. My increasingly slow pace wasn't going to win any endorsements at the Tour de France. I gritted my teeth and kept going anyway.

Soon the houses stopped and the trees closed in. I was almost to the summit. That's when I encountered the 400-pound mama bear and cub.

Usually on my rides across rural New England I encounter fox, deer or moose. Harmless creatures. Dogs sometimes chased me. But I'd never been chased before by hungry black bears.

The bears loped out of the woods and were halfway across the road when the mama bear must have heard me. She stopped and did a double take. We were only about twenty feet apart.

Fortunately, I scared the bears more than they scared me. I was breathing hard, with a terrible grimace of pain on my face. The adult bear must have thought, "Holy twigs and blueberries, that guy looks mean!" because she fled into a grove of apple trees on the far side of the road. The little cub scurried after her.

I continued to the top and turned around only to meet four more bears on the way back down. Mama bear must have summoned reinforcements.

This time the bears ambled across the road, in no hurry to get out of the way. I decided to slow down and let them cross at their leisure rather than charging at them at 40 mph. They appreciated my gesture and decided not to eat me.

My adventures weren't over yet. Back on the flats, I crossed paths with a creature even scarier than bears. I'm still not sure what it was. Perhaps just a hawk or an eagle, but I'll never know for sure. All I ever saw was the creature's shadow. It had wings—big wings. The shadow of the flying monster darkened the sky. Glancing back over my shoulder into the sun, I blinked, shut my eyes, and turned my head away. Whatever was up there was flying low, directly between me and the sun. Gazing down, I could see the silhouette of wings, enormous wings, seeming to sprout from my own shadow's back. Whatever the animal was, it flew right overhead.

For one frightful instant I feared I was going to be eaten by a pterodactyl. I imagined the creature clasping me in its talons, bicycle and all, and carting me off to some mountain aerie for dinner.

I didn't want to be on the menu. I peddled faster. Geez, I thought, first bears, now ancient, predatory reptiles. What's next? All I wanted was to get home, where it was safe.

Watch out Lance Armstrong. Turns out I'm a world class athlete when being chased by bears and toothy, flying reptiles.

I finished my ride in record time.

Two Wheels Good
A True Story

Once I had a little car.
It never traveled very far.
On every trip I'd end up towed.
I rode my bike, unless it snowed.
My car broke down again today.
There's only one thing left to say.
My bike has never made me sad.
Two wheels good...
        Four wheels bad.

Up, Up, and Away

SPRING IS HERE, THE ICE has melted, and the highway department has finally gotten around to cleaning up the road salt and sand. At last I can hop on my bike and pedal away.

I like riding uphill, especially now. The leaves are barely budding, so distant vistas open through the trees. I climb higher, following a ridgeline street. Nestled in the valley below, the houses and buildings of Berlin, New Hampshire shrink to tiny, toy-like proportions. Up here it almost feels more like flying than riding— like Superman soaring above Metropolis.

I slow to drink some water and admire the view. A house stands just down the road, and a dog—a golden retriever—plays in the yard. The dog has a chew toy, a small tire from a Tonka truck. The dog shakes his head, the tire slips out, lands on its edge, and starts rolling. Faster, faster, faster. That tire isn't going to stop. It's a good mile before the road levels off.

On my bike, I zoom to the rescue. The dog seems happy to get his chew toy back.

On the other side of town, at the top of a long, steep street, more heroics are called for. I'm coasting back down the street after a hard, fast climb when I pass a yard where a boy and his father are playing with a beach ball. The boy kicks the ball and—

oops! It rolls into the street and starts bouncing downhill, picking up speed. *Boing! Boing! Boing!* It looks like one of those menacing killer spheres from the TV show *The Prisoner*, descending on the helpless village below.

I barely manage to chase the ball down on my bike. Tucking it under one arm, I return it to the yard from which it tried to escape.

That's enough rescues for one day. But who knows what tomorrow will bring?

Whatever happens, I'll be ready. Helmet, check. Sunglasses, check. Bicycle tires fully inflated, check. All I need now is a secret identity and a cape. I can be a superhero. Returner of Runaway Toys, Protector of Golden Retrievers. Look! Up in the sky! It's a bird. It's a plane. It's...me, defending the sleepy village below from things that go *boing boing boing*.

Armchair Travelers

BOOKS ARE LIKE PASSPORTS TO *new countries, new worlds. Here are reviews of a few books that keep getting reread.*

The Winds of War, by Herman Wouk

IMAGINE STARVING TO DEATH in a snowy, besieged Leningrad, licking the glue off wallpaper for nutrients. Imagine watching human beings, your neighbors, herded like cattle onto trains, en route to a clouded fate about which you and they have heard terrible rumors you cannot quite believe. In Herman Wouk's *The Winds of War* and its sequel *War and Remembrance*, these scenes from World War II seem vividly, shockingly real. Wouk takes you places you'd never want to go but somehow can't stop reading about.

Two of Wouk's own characters sum up the appeal of these books. In one scene, Victor Henry, a U.S. naval officer on a Lend-Lease mission to the Soviet Union, and Pamela Tudsbury, daughter and assistant of a British journalist, witness a tank battle close to Moscow. The Germans are winning. The war won't end anytime soon. That's bad news, but Pamela remarks:

> "...I felt relieved. Relieved! What kind of mad reaction was that?"
>
> "Well, the war's something different, while it lasts." Victor Henry gestured at the angry yellow flare-ups on the black western clouds. "The expensive fireworks—the travel to strange places—"
>
> "The interesting company," Pam said.
>
> "Yes, Pam. The interesting company."

The Winds of War and its sequel introduce you to characters you come to know and care about, then follow them around the world from 1939 to 1945. This is more than a book of battles and death. It's a story full of politics (a French Zionist smuggles Jewish refugees to Palestine, Roosevelt maneuvers around an isolationist Congress to convoy supplies through U-Boat infested waters to Britain), long-distance love affairs, cultural clashes, and ordinary people coping with extraordinary hardships.

Each time I reread these books they remind me a little of *The Lord of the Rings*. Both are world-spanning travel epics revolving around a war. In both, the protagonists start out together in a peaceful, naïve, untouched land (The Shire and the United States 1939) but then journey to nations where dark clouds gather. Natalie and Aaron more or less travel into Mordor, with Werner Beck as their own personal Gollum. Stalingrad is the Siege of Gondor, with Lend-Lease like Rohan riding to the rescue. And so forth. In the end, the survivors all gather together again, greatly changed-some with wounds that won't completely heal.

The Lord of the Rings:
Hiking in Tolkien's Middle Earth

THE LAST THING THE WORLD needs is another review of *The Lord of the Rings*. Here's one anyway.

The first time I read Tolkien, the mushroom/Bombadil chapters made my eyes glaze over. The hobbits just kept walking and talking and—oh, look! A shrub! And now it's raining! How exciting. I skimmed ahead until they got to Bree.

I also remember (with some amusement) closing the book soon after Mt. Doom erupted and Aragorn's army stood victorious at the gates of Mordor. Obviously the story was over, right? Sure, there were three or four more chapters. But to my ten-year-old eyes they looked like more mushroom/Bombadil filler. It wasn't until my second reading of *The Lord of the Rings* that I discovered what is now my favorite chapter, "The Scouring of the Shire."

"Scouring" isn't just my favorite chapter; it is, in my opinion, the whole point of the book. For the first time, the hobbits must battle an enemy with no help from wizards, rangers, elves, or magic. Gandalf himself explains as he and the hobbits near the troubled Shire:

> "Well, we've got you with us," said Merry, "so things will soon be cleared up."
>
> "I am with you at present," said Gandalf, "but soon I shall not be. I am not coming to the Shire. You must settle its affairs yourselves; that is what you've been trained for."

The hobbits left the Shire as children, naïve and dependent on others. They returned as adults.

By now I've read *The Lord of the Rings* enough times to know the plot backward and forward. Yet I keep rereading it. The first couple readings I was eager to press on, to find out what happens next. I tended to skim over the poems and songs. They got in the way of the action. Now I enjoy these parts, too. I can read more slowly, carefully, savoring all the depth and detail of Middle Earth.

As an avid hiker, I get a chuckle out of imagining Tolkien writing a very different kind of book. *A Walk in the Shire*, perhaps. Or *The Appalachian Mountain Club Guide to Hiking Trails in the Old Forest*. "Short cuts make long delays" is good advice in any guidebook. Perhaps the next *AMC Guide to the Mountains of Mordor* could include a warning about poorly marked trails near Cirith Ungol Notch. Several hikers have reported getting lost there and being eaten by spiders.

Recently I reread Tolkien for the umpteenth time. I finally learned to enjoy the "mushroom and Tom Bombadil" sections, with the emphasis on the scenery. I was in no hurry to get to Rivendell; I'd been there umpteen times before. So I deliberately slowed down and hiked with the hobbits through the woods of the Shire, under the dense canopy of the Old Forest, and across the cold, foggy Downs-places I used to hurry through, scarcely glancing at the trees and rivers and wide-open spaces all around me. This time, I actually stopped to visit Goldberry, where before I'd always rushed past rudely without much more than a quick "hello."

The appeal of this epic tale isn't the writing; it's the rich detail and history of the world Tolkien created. Reading the *Lord of the Rings* is like putting on your hiking boots and taking a stroll in Middle Earth.

Replay, by Ken Grimwood

A FORTY-SOMETHING MAN WITH an unhappy marriage and a job he despises feels a sudden pain in his chest, which he assumes is a heart attack. He collapses. When he wakes up, he's not in a hospital bed—he's lying on his back in a college dorm room. A vaguely familiar-looking college dorm room. He looks in a mirror and he sees himself—at age 18.

This is a book full of intriguing questions. What if you could relive your life? Would you have the same friends, choose the same career, marry the same person? What if you knew everything that was going to happen for the next twenty years? Yet you can barely remember your college friends' names, or what courses you're supposed to be taking, or what happened "yesterday." What do you do? What is it like to interact with parents and teachers when you're actually older than they are? Could you change history? Could you, say, stop the Kennedy assassination? What would happen if you tried?

Every few years I reread this book and enjoy it every time. It's amusing when the main character can't find anything but "oldies" on the radio. In fact, he can't even find the FM dial.

The culture shock of going suddenly from the 1980s back to the early 1960s is part of what makes the book so interesting. I wish the author, or anyone else, would write a sequel set two decades later. It would be fascinating to watch a character who has seen the end of the Cold War, the explosion of the Internet and the home computer market, the Challenger and Columbia disasters, September 11, *etc.*, suddenly thrust back into 1979.

The Cat with Ten Lives

BLACKIE THE CAT WAS BORN on the night of the Democratic National Convention in 1984. During his kitten years, Blackie roamed the countryside, stalking mice in distant cornfields and climbing over tall hills for adventure. After each long journey, he'd reappear as if by magic on our living-room sofa, curled up in front of the wood stove for a well-deserved nap.

When one of our distant neighbors reported seeing a stray cat in his alfalfa fields, I suspected it was Blackie. Sure enough, this "stray" had a snowy white belly and a tuft of white on his chin. It was Blackie, miles from home.

As years passed, he continued to wander across the county. But he soon learned a hard lesson: Always look and listen before running across a road. At age five, he was hit by a pickup truck. Somehow, he suffered nothing worse than a broken nose.

A year or so later, Blackie used up yet another life. He disappeared during a January blizzard; we thought he'd finally met his end. How could a small cat possibly walk through ten-foot snowdrifts or survive night after night in bone-chilling sub-zero temperatures?

Three days after the blizzard ended, we heard a noise at the door. There he was, sitting on the back porch, patiently tapping the back door with his paw.

Once inside, he gobbled down a bowl of cat food and milk, then spent the entire afternoon huddled in front of the wood stove. The next day, he insisted on going right back outside into winter's raw grip.

His latest caper ought to have finished him for sure. "He's lucky to be alive," our vet told us, shaking his head in amazement. Blackie had been missing for three days when he suddenly crawled up onto the porch, bloody and battered. He meowed pitifully. His sleek black fur was streaked with blood. Mucus glued shut his eyes. Black flies festered in his wounds. He suffered from a broken leg and shattered jaw.

Blinded and in pain, he somehow had stumbled across many miles back to our door. But his pulse was still strong.

"He must have really wanted to live," our vet said. We think he was hit by a tractor or a baler in a far-off field.

After several weeks of recovery, the metal wires were removed from Blackie's jaw. With the help of some foul-tasting medicine, his eyes cleared and his vision returned to normal. He began following us around the house despite being slowed by his wounded leg.

At the veterinarian's office, Blackie has become sort of a legend—the cat that wouldn't die. And his fame has spread beyond the hospital walls.

Not long after his recovery, my mother was introduced to someone in a grocery store as "Blackie's owner." A family friend reports that he was asked by a stranger, "You know Blackie, don't you?"

Will Blackie ever recover and be the same as before? No one knows. But one thing is certain. Even though he is a normal-sized cat, Blackie possesses the heart and mind of a mountain lion.

Various Thumping Arguments

CALEB KELLOGG WAS A POOR equestrian and a worse writer.

In one painfully tongue-twisting run-on sentence (which I won't inflict upon you here) he advised people to keep journals. His own journal, he claimed, had improved his memory and enhanced his powers of observation, allowing him to record events with "more accuracy and correctness."

Mercifully for readers, his writing style improved somewhat. His horse-riding skills did not.

At 2 P.M. on a cold November day in 1824, eighteen-year-old Caleb mounted a yellow pony and set out on a journey alone from Vermont to Canada. The animal promptly bucked and threw him off.

"After being thrown in an attempt to get on I proceeded at a moderate pace with the expectation of reaching Milton tonight. At the distance of a few miles, on my right, the snow white summits of Mansfield Mountain and Camel's Rump [today called Camel's Hump] reared their heads to the clouds. The air was cold and everything showed that winter was fast approaching.

"Various thoughts occupied my mind as I proceeded leisurely along until I was roused from my reflections when within about ½ mile from Burlington—by my nag's refusing to proceed. After various thumping arguments had been used on my part he summed up the whole and gave me his opinion on the subject by lying or falling down in the road. When I attempted to dismount she assisted me in operation by rising so suddenly that she threw me prostrate on the earth and I was under the necessity of trudging to Burlington on foot."

Note how Caleb's mount changes gender from one sentence to the next. So much for "accuracy and correctness."

Two more days of riding (and occasional unplanned walking) followed. The roads changed from "tolerable good" to "very bad."

Caleb wrote, "Necessity again compelled me to mount my pony and journey through a snowstorm to Canada. I was under the necessity of getting a shoe set on my horse which a conscientious young blacksmith was so good as to accommodate me.

"The wind was in the South and a heavy damp snow continued to fall during the day. About 2 miles from Highgate Falls I met a man riding leisurely along and after riding about a mile I met a man riding very rapidly in pursuit—what the object was, I do not know."

Caleb next lost his way, galloped five miles down the wrong road, and stopped several times to ask for directions. Late that afternoon, with the sun threatening to set, he finally reached the boundary between the U.S. and Canada. "This was the first time I had ever left my native country and entered the Dominions & never before had known the feelings of a person entering another country," he said. His nag, properly shod, gave no more trouble and was not mentioned again.

Only a few typewritten pages of Caleb Kellogg's journal survive. They were put into legible form by an anonymous typist in the 1930s before the originals crumbled to dust, and now sit in a dusty, rarely-opened box at the Vermont Historical Society in Barre, Vermont.

In a somewhat less dusty corner of the Bennington Museum's library sits the humorously self-deprecating journal of another 19th century Vermonter, farmer Hiram Harwood. Like Kellogg, Hiram was not above using the occasional "thumping argument" on his beasts of burden. One day he struck a young cow in anger—and immediately regretted the violent impulse. (The animal barely noticed the blow, but Hiram's hand throbbed with pain for the next three days.)

Hiram endured more agony each time he hitched up his horses to the wagon and journeyed into town. When snow melted and the ground thawed, the muddy roads took their toll on travelers. Summertime roads were so rutty that one historian claimed the jolting motion of a wagon could "churn cream to butter."

During one half-mile trip by wagon into Bennington, each bounce and bump caused Hiram's father Benjamin to yell "loud enough to be heard 2 miles." Benjamin quieted as the trip proceeded, but "constantly kept groaning until he alighted from the jostling vehicle."

Unfortunately for Hiram and his father, the typical wagon of the early 1800s did not come equipped with much of a suspension system. Steel springs made poor shock absorbers. Innovations such as thoroughbraces—thick leather straps placed under the body of the wagon—were years in the future. Thoroughbraces would give wagons and stagecoaches a gentler front-and-back rocking motion; Mark Twain once described the sensation as riding in "a cradle on wheels." But such comfort was denied to Hiram and his groaning dad.

A Farmer's Almanac

"MURDER! MURDER! MURDER!" the children shouted. "Do run, run, run. Mr. Harwood, do run!"

It was Thursday, April 30, 1812, in Bennington, Vermont. Hiram Harwood and his father Benjamin were plowing a meadow near their neighbor Mr. Brown's property. The weather was fine, the sun just starting to sink toward the still-leafless trees in the late afternoon. Shadows slowly lengthened across the ground, and Hiram and Benjamin hurried to finish their work.

Suddenly they heard cries, panicked voices of an unknown number of women and children. The hubbub came from just over the ridge. People were calling their names. Hiram and Benjamin dropped their tools and ran to see what was the fuss was about.

Hiram outpaced his father and soon saw ahead "the theatre of action." Young children urged him on. "Do run, run, run. Mr. Harwood, do run!"

Hiram "hastened with additional speed up to the ground which gave birth to this confused noise." For all he knew, he was about to catch an actual murderer in the act.

What he saw astonished him. "I beheld the heads of two families clenched together, scratching, biting and pulling each other by the hair with bloody hands and faces." He compared

84

them to two bears fighting. "I did not wait long to witness so disgusting a scene," he wrote. He seized the shoulders of the top man and tried to haul him off. But the "two bears" were intent on ripping out each other's throats, and Hiram by himself failed to separate them.

His father, out of breath, arrived to help. Together they managed to "succeed in quelling the squabble." In his diary, Hiram made no mention of what the fight was about, just that he and his father negotiated a truce. And then, as if nothing had happened, they "returned again to our business" in the fields.

Hiram wasn't used to brawling with his neighbors. But squabbling with his own family, particularly his father, was an everyday occurrence.

"I get out of patience with him—and he with himself," Benjamin once said of Hiram. The elder Harwood called his son "a poor recommendation for a young man of 22." He added, "I have a hope for him, but, I confess, it rests on a sandy foundation."

To help cure Hiram of his lazy, lackadaisical habits, Benjamin assigned his son an extra chore: writing once a day in the family diary.

The Harwood family diary a time machine. Each page transports the reader back across a gap of almost two centuries, revealing what Hiram saw and heard—and thought and felt—as he stepped in cowhide boots and farmer's overalls across the agrarian landscape of early nineteenth-century Vermont.

"Traversed the fields and meadows to avoid mud and company," he wrote one afternoon. In a snapshot of farming life, Hiram noted how he greeted a friend and "shook him by a polluted hand." Hiram had just been spreading manure as fertilizer on the potato fields.

The diary tells as much about Hiram and his personality as

about the time and place in which he lived. "In a fit of anger this morning struck a young calf in such a way as to lame my hand & wrist several days," he once admitted.

"Must I bear witness against myself – of my folly, ignorance and sloth?" he wondered. "Yes, perhaps by keeping these things in remembrance, I shall learn to shun some of the snares that, without admonition, I might heedlessly fall into. I certainly desire to improve in every undertaking that I may pursue."

For the next several years, cheerful confessions of folly and sloth filled pages, but there was scant evidence of any improvement in his work ethic. At sunset on a June day in 1815, he played his flute outdoors, neglecting his chores. The sheep wandered, and his grandfather, who had been weighing the fleece, became "tired and full of vexation."

Hiram's grandfather quizzed the young man "in a hard tone" as to why he was dawdling, then ordered him to bring up the sheep before nightfall.

"I obeyed orders," wrote Hiram—but he took his flute with him. The sun had set by the time he found the sheep. He herded them into the lane, but he himself "played and marched slowly." The sheep raced on ahead, until a coyote spooked them and they fled to the far corner of a distant pasture. Hiram, far behind, didn't even notice. He was still playing his flute. It was his neighbor Locke who leaped over the fence to herd the sheep away.

Hiram came up the path at last. First he saw Locke. Then he saw the sheep. Then he saw that he was late and in trouble. "Your father will whip you for not being more expeditious," his friend Locke warned him."

Hiram was untroubled. "I played Yankee Doodle and deliberately marched on." When he caught up with his father, he helped gather the flock. All the while his father Benjamin was silent with rage.

Finally, the task done, Benjamin turned to him. "If you had been a boy," he said, "you would have had a fine shaking." Grandfather, while waiting, had taken cold. "I would try to be a boy or a man," said Benjamin Harwood. "I would be one or the other."

Later, Hiram regretted his childishness that day and recorded the incident in the diary for all to see. "This anecdote reflects disgrace on its author," he wrote. He added, "Amen, says the reader or hearer."

Clueless

WHEN THE WIDOW JONES SCREAMED, her prim mouth rounded into a horrified little 'o'. "Another guest dead! And at dinner, too!" As a proper hostess, she knew that dead people belonged in the ground, not at the dinner table—not even when dressed in a suit and tie.

The butler and Mrs Jones' two surviving guests fidgeted in a corner of the room, equally alarmed.

Detective Joe Thicke stood over the body. He lifted off the bloody toupee, studied it carefully. "Hmmm," he said. "This man appears to be dead." Quickly he verified his hypothesis by failing to find the dead man's pulse.

Next, he scrutinized the four suspects. Of the four, the white-faced widow and her butler appeared the most upset. But the two young men in blue blazers seemed quite relaxed—too relaxed. They had already consumed a fair share of liquor, and both still sipped from their glasses.

"Lady and gentlemen," said Detective Thicke. "And you too, butler-boy. Today—" Suddenly the two gentlemen clinked their glasses together. "—today a murder has taken place! One of the people in this room is a killer!"

Joe nudged the corpse over with his foot, revealing a long,

bloody, yellow pencil buried almost up to the eraser in the dead man's throat.

"You know," mumbled one of the intoxicated youths, "I always thought there would be less crime if nothing were illegal."

Joe paused, blinked, and rubbed his masculine jaw. "Yes, quite." Could one of these drunks be the criminal? No, their faces were just too honest.

Joe studied his third suspect, the widow. Not bad, he thought, but a little too plump. And her aristocratic nose wasn't to his taste.

The bald butler was next in line. The old fellow held a box of eleven freshly sharpened pencils in his white gloved hands. Joe observed that the box had room for one more pencil. Hmm, what could have become of it?

Aha! Suddenly Joe saw a clue. Two bloody splotches stained the Persian rug near where the young gentlemen stood. Joe scratched his chin and wondered aloud, "Hmm, two bloodstains..."

"To bloodstains!" toasted the young men. *Clink* went the glasses.

"Yes," said Joe. "Two bloodstains right there on the carpet behind you. Can you explain them?"

All four suspects stared at him, blinking in bewilderment. "You're crazy!" screamed the widow.

She must still be in shock, thought Joe. "People," he said, "this case is solved. The butler did it, in the study, with the revolver...I mean the pencil!"

Finally the shock wore off Widow Jones and her guests. But the butler spoke up first. "But...but...you killed that man," he sputtered, pointing a bony finger at Detective Joe. "You walked in, asked to borrow a pencil, then stabbed that poor man in the throat. You're insane!" The others nodded in cautious agreement. "Far out," said one of the drunks.

"You could be right," Joe told the butler. "The only way to prove your story is to check the pencil for fingerprints. I shall do so." Joe reached down to pluck the pencil from the victim's throat. With his other hand, he pulled a silk cloth from his vest pocket and used it to wipe the pencil clean. Then he examined the pencil.

"No," said Joe. "I'm afraid the killer was smart enough to wipe the pencil clean. And since you, butler-boy, are wearing gloves, only you could have done that."

The widow protested. "But you just wiped it with that cloth!"

"What cloth?" asked Joe, putting it back in his pocket.

"But we all saw you kill him!"

"Well," said Joe, "four eyewitnesses. Five, since in all honesty I did see myself commit the murder." He strode across the room toward the widow's musical instrument collection, where he nervously began to open and close a violin case. "It's an open and shut case," he said. "As an officer of the law, it's my duty to arrest this dangerous killer, me. I should be considered armed and dangerous. Do you?"

"What?" came a chorus of four voices.

"Do you consider me armed and dangerous?"

"Oh, certainly, sir," said the butler.

"Well," said Joe. "I shall now take the defendant to jail. Good day!" With a curt nod, Joe fled through the open window.

A Morning for Artists and Preachers

A PRICKLY PAIN SPREAD ACROSS Phil's chest, but he suffered in silence. He wouldn't cry for help. He still had his pride, after all. That young woman, Sally, treated him like a brittle vase that needed keeping in a box. She'd just fuss and worry if she knew.

Phil lay motionless on the couch, letting the dust of Sunday morning settle all around him. His brown eyes hid under drowsy, half-closed eyelids. He faced the single window, a large glass pane peering down at the mountain and the little village lodged in its shadow.

The mountain cast a dark, ironic reflection on the room's opposite wall, where a painting hung like a mirror. Painted hilltops stood in the distance, with a hamlet squeezed between the valley walls. From out of the painted village protruded a church's tall steeple, a spike thrust deep into the belly of a cloud.

In the real village far below, two such steeples lifted in competition. Phil had purposely built his house high on the side of the valley, to avoid looking up at those monoliths each Sunday.

From his perch on the couch, Phil could see a long line of hills rolling toward a gentle morning blue. The mountain's rocky peak, stripped of trees, caught the sunlight and glittered. The clouds were harmless clumps of white wool. Closer, Phil could see a corner of his shed, the sturdy tool house he'd built last summer. He'd been working on the shed three days ago when the pains first hit him, like branches of thorns twisting in his ribs. His lungs writhed, sucking in each breath. He fell against the shed wall, drinking sweet, cold air, letting the breezes flush out his lungs.

But he never told Sally, his niece; she'd have heckled him each time he raised an arm, strapped him to a bed while autumn wasted away. Already she tried to keep him from the hardest chores, or else sent her husband, Robert, to help. Whenever she brought water and biscuits at noon, he could tell it was just to keep an eye on him, to make sure he hadn't fallen or broken a bone. She was always watching, that one. He could feel her eyes on his back, staring out the window while he hammered nails into the boards.

A curtain rod cast a shadow on the floor, a long, thin beam that cut across Phil's knees. When the wind blew in, this shadow swung across the floor, back and forth, like the boom of a ship.

The room was shaped like a long thin rectangle, a box of stark boards holding a desk, a couch, a wardrobe, and a single shelf of books. A wide, pale oval stained the floor where the rug had been ripped away, exposing the white wood beneath. The open window filled one end, the grim painting the other.

Phil remembered that new pastor down in the village—though it wasn't fair to call him new, for he'd been toting his Bible around the valley for twelve years now. That *young* pastor had once sat on this very couch and proclaimed the painting a perfect example of why artists should go to church more often. The painting's sky was dimly lit by a sharp slice of waxing moon, and the deep purple clouds of night coiled like a whip over the hilltops. Dark, stunted mounds rolled across the painting's horizon. The painting was a deep, elfin reflection of the true valley outside, and Phil preferred it to the real thing. It was finished, perfected.

The pastor, like a good shepherd, had come to bring Phil down off the mountain nearly a decade ago. He had spoken first to Phil's father, who was old and bitter. He could tell by the way the man peered around every corner, looking for signs of the Devil's mischief.

His father had asked him to come back home, for he was dying—that was the pastor's message. But Phil had heard it all before. "You never come to see me," said his father on one of Phil's weekly visits. He spoke those words at the dinner table eight years ago; three candles and a rigid, brass crucifix stood on the table between them.

"How can you be so unmindful of your duty? Will you leave me to die alone?"

That, thought Phil, was the reason he had left.

Now he lay flat on his couch looking down on the village buried in evergreens at the foot of the valley. He had errands to run in town, but it was a long walk down. They could wait. The sofa's warmth penetrated his shirt, caressing his skin. The air was chill. Moving out the carpet had opened up a crack for the November wind—and that had to be fixed before Sal and Robert noticed.

The sun, now risen over the mountain, tossed golden light into Phil's eyes. He tried to blink, but his lids refused to move. On his chin, a beardful of gray whiskers dried and curled. Streaks of dust and dirt on the window cast a net of tiny shadows against the walls, the ceiling, the floor. The sight of these black dots— imperfections all of them—irritated Phil, for they were reminders that the windows needed washing.

Phil felt proud of the big window in his study, for he was lucky to have carried so large a sheet of glass up the hill. But the chore of cleaning could wait till he got back from town.

A fat black book sat atop his desk in a corner of the room, where the direct rays of the sun bit into it. Phil felt a sudden urge to rescue it from its wooden island in the sun.

He always kept books in the shade, save for now and again when he took one from the shelf and left it lying about. His bookcase, shielded by the taller wardrobe, was immune to the sun's rays. He had positioned it just so, since the sun blistered his pale skin a painful crimson, and he feared it would do the same to the crisp white paper. His books were valuable; with every trip down to Boston, he added to their number.

The bookshelf was crowded. To make room for new volumes, Phil had to push open new spaces with his hand. Smaller texts soon forfeited their places and lay horizontally across the spines of their larger neighbors. An uneven bed, he thought, like the cross-section of a city, square and jagged.

But the black book was larger than most, with an intimidating spine that dwarfed its fellows. It was an anthology of sorts: *Literature of the Puritan Culture.* A yellow-brown stain splattered across its cover, and Phil remembered spilling his coffee at breakfast, three or four days ago—he couldn't remember exactly when or how.

The couch's cushions felt very warm on his back, and the sunlight was like a blanket above him. How long since he had last lain down like this, just resting?

He had nearly dozed off when the door swung quietly inward. Sally's feet tracked softly across the day's dust. Her eyes passed over him, anxiously he thought, but she didn't speak. Phil started to open his mouth, but his tongue felt stiff and cold and refused to stir.

Sally turned away from him, walking over to the desk. A single book rested on top. Now hadn't he just put that book away?

But this was a smaller book, brown and leather-bound. Of

course—the pastor's book. Sally snatched it up, glancing uncertainly at the spine. She nudged open a space for it on the bookcase and straightened out the others.

Damn it all, thought Phil, she didn't have to do all that. She had enough to take care of without fussing over his books. That much, at least, he could still do himself.

Sally cast her eyes at the curtain, the walls, anywhere but at Phil. She strode across the room, pulled the curtain closed. Her lips trembled as if she had something to say but didn't know where to start.

Of course. They had quarreled last night. Phil recalled shouting, though not what about. He'd shouted for her, or at her, but Robert had come instead. He was sorry about that, for he never shouted. Never. Not even when a side of roof fell on him, back when the house was going up years ago—he'd bit his tongue, held back the screams, and was proud of that. When Berta came out to give him a drink, like she always did, the two of them had lifted it off.

Though he wanted to talk to Sal, he could not start this conversation, for he was unsure which of them should apologize. This house would be hers soon. Robert's too; that couldn't be helped. They had both come when he'd written, made the trip from Ashboro, two valleys over. Sally was his last relative in this world, besides a cousin way off in New York.

Still she ignored him. She bent down and groped with her hands in the wardrobe, searching for something. For a minute she rummaged through the drawers, then stood up sharply, as if bitten or stung. She turned around, caught Phil's eye. Whatever she saw there made her run from the room, slamming the door rudely behind her.

Now Phil had had enough of this game. All morning, Sally kept looking in on him, but she never spoke. He had no time to stay and wait for her. There were things to do, a trip to town to make. When he returned, there would be time enough to talk. They had never really talked, he knew, not about important things. That was why he had asked her to come—to talk, while there was still time.

The book Sally had held—the pastor's book—was a Bible, its cover worn a dull brown with black flaps curled up along the edges from always being stuffed in and out of the pastor's coat pocket. The priest had come to argue three days ago, and he had left the Bible on the desk, so that Phil would at least need to touch it to move it aside. "Take the time to read it, Phil," were the pastor's parting words. "You've read everything else."

Phil had laughed, shown him the door. "I don't need your book. I've enough of my own."

The pastor had hiked up the mountain for a reason, like Moses in search of God. But he had found Phil instead. Phil didn't like guests who tossed their chatter in the air and their morals in his face. In town, folks called him the Heathen—behind his back, of course, where he could hear it only in whispers. They mocked his isolated life in his cabin on the hill, but were glad enough to see him whenever the rain leaked on their heads through the roof of the church. He had spent more time working on that roof with a hammer than most folk spent kneeling inside. If the sound of their prayers filtered up through the ceiling, he pounded the noise away with a hammer, driving a nail through the preacher's sermon. He had stopped to listen to the singing, though.

"Haven't seen you lately, Phil," the pastor had said, hooking his coat on the rack like he meant to stay a while.

"Nope. Been busy." He didn't offer the man a seat, but dipped a cold drink from the bucket, just up from the well. Townsfolk weren't used to climbing; there was a strain in the pastor's hurried breaths, a pasty sweat on his brow.

The pastor gulped down the water gladly, mumbled a word of

thanks. Phil took a sip himself. They were quiet for a time, letting the water cool them.

The pastor spoke first. That was his job—breaking silence. "We had hoped you'd help us with the door on the new church. Before winter comes. The nights are getting long, you know."

Phil wandered towards his study, expecting the priest to follow. "I'm busy with my own doors. I get the worst of the weather up here." He sat on the couch, offered the priest a chair with a wave of his hand. "You don't really need a new church. The old one's enough trouble, down in a rut where the water rots the wood."

The pastor's eyes absorbed the titles in Phil's bookcase. He fumbled with his drinking cup. "How have you been, Phil? Still active?"

Phil pointed an aggressive finger. "I'm just fine, thank you, and I don't need some spokesman from the village fussing about my health." He saw a faint smile twitch on the younger man's face—a sign that he was being humored. "Sally does enough fussing as it is. Her husband, too."

"Will your niece stay with you for the winter?"

"Maybe. Is it any of your affair?" Phil stared into the painting, hanging behind the pastor. From this angle, the priest's forehead interrupted the flow of dark hills and blotted out the village entirely.

"We're worried about you, Phil. Everyone appreciates what you've done for them, and we'd hate to see you break your neck on the ice coming down for a visit."

"I can take care of myself as well as ever."

"Can you? The Parkers told me at church it's been three weeks and you haven't stopped by, not even for dinner. You used to help them every week, fixing that barn that the storm blew in."

"I've been busy, like I said. Can't take care of everybody, like you do."

Later, Phil had called Christ a busybody, which set the pastor coughing, red-faced. People never spoke like that to a priest, not if they lived in town and had to see him every day.

The pastor had taken out his little book, pointing it like a weapon. He placed it right in the middle of the desk when he rose to go. But that was days ago, soon after Sally had come. Sally, too, had been hounding him to go to church, as if it was an urgent chore that needed doing before the first snowfall. Phil decided instead that making a windbreak was more important.

The sun hung outside the window. Its warmth made Phil feel sleepy, though he usually went without an afternoon nap. But getting that shed up had drained him; he'd earned his rest.

He drowsed off and stayed asleep until loud voices started drumming on his ears. Sal and Robert were shouting just outside the door. Couldn't they keep their quarrels to themselves? It was bad enough that he had shouted at Sally last night, yelled something. What was this about, now?

Phil heard the drawers in the kitchen suddenly yanked open and slammed closed all at once, a frenzied racket of wood hitting wood. What was Sally looking for?

Then the slamming stopped. Phil heard Robert speak faintly, "...tomorrow...the pastor will...." That was all. Robert's voice was soft, smothered by the thick door to the study, which made shouts sound like whispers. He'd built the door that way on purpose, to keep out noise, back when Berta used to bang on the pots at every meal.

"If you can't stand his damn black eyes, keep out of the room!" These acid words from Robert sounded crisp and clear, right outside the door. Phil guessed they were talking about him. Robert never could look him eye to eye.

Sal was crying now, not loud, but he could hear it through the door. He heard Robert mutter some comforting babble about being sorry.

Phil stiffened his jaw, furious. He didn't have to stand for this in his own house; he get up and set things straight.

Almost Phil set a foot on the floor. But his legs felt sluggish, weighted down.

Sal and Robert were quiet now. He'd heard Robert apologize. It wouldn't do to get involved. And he felt so...weary, reluctant to stir from the warm cushions.

Again, the sound of a drawer slammed shut penetrated the door. But Phil could not move.

He tried to close his eyes, but sleep was beyond him now. He felt lazy yet alert. No good working in this state of mind. Soon he would have to go to town, see the pastor about that big door.

He gazed into the stunted mounds of the painting, where the thick oil made the twilight churn wildly. It was a good painting, that, and he hoped Sal would take care of it when it came to be hers. He couldn't live forever. The pastor, the old one, not that new import from Boston, the pastor had said—

The door swung open. Sally stood there, her face red, her swollen hands coiled around an old blanket sewn in a pattern of white diamonds set against black cloth. Now where had she found that old thing? Her grandmother had knitted it in the bad winter of '81, the same year she took ill and was set to rest in the cemetery behind the church. Two weeks of fierce snow had walled in their house in the village, but his father had made him dig a way out, so they could go to church. He remembered the blanket on father's bed in winter, when—

Sal ran to him. He uttered no cry of surprise, for there was no time. She swooped over him; the black cloth fluttered in the air, falling upon him. It settled on his face and he somehow he couldn't lift a hand to fend it off. The world blackened.

As Sally covered his face and body with the shroud, he felt again the sharp pain in his chest, the same ache that had awakened him last night, the pain that, for the first time in his life, had made him swallow his pride and scream.

Lonely Stanza

The music lasts
a short while only.
Then all is quiet.
Some remember the music,
but it does not play again.

Waves

A lidless eye
blinks twilight through the trees.

A gray tide
erases wet feet running

like children along the shoreline
in the morning. It is evening;

the beach is bare.
There is no one here.

Sunbeams breach the branches
Scattering red rays;

Golden bulbs ignite
on the tops of waves.

A thinning strip of sand
exists in the midst

of a bridge of wet wind
blowing land to sea, sea to land.

The slag of a sandcastle
sinks like Atlantis

as the tidewater slaps its ruins
until, each evening,

the flatland of morning
is achieved. The beach now waits

for the dent
of the first fallen foot.

Fisherman's Bane

AN OLD FISHERMAN LIVED ALONE in a cave, a crevasse ripped open by the twitching of fault lines. Deep inside his cave, a shallow stream surfaced briefly, forming a pool before it trickled under the rocks. He called this puddle "the sink," and sipped its thin, rusty waters twice a day.

Moisture glistened and clung to the cave's walls, and often he pressed the dry skin of his forehead against the cool stone after a day's work in the sun. The rest of his face was hairy. White whiskers drooped to his waist, dripping moisture from a dip in the sink.

Outside, where he worked, all water had long since burned away in the penetrating heat of the sun. The sky was no longer blue. Dawn cast a fierce red flame across the eastern skyline, where the sands of a dead ocean nudged against the base of the mountains. Each day, at sunrise, the old man walked down to shore to set his lines. But nothing tugged on the bait, for the brittle bones of fish lay very still, buried by the drifting dunes.

Deep in the man's mind, he saw a picture of an ocean, blue and alive. Liquid waves splashed against the sand and sent cold, white foam rolling up the shore, washing the wet sand from his feet. Then the ocean pulled back with a hushed growl, only to surge forward, again and again. Brisk morning air flushed his cheeks with life, and a salty spray slapped playfully at his face to knock the sleep from his crusty eyes.

All along the winding shore, amid crests of breaking waves, tall crags protruded above the water like the fingers of giant Poseidon reaching up from the depths. Between these monoliths people swam or walked or fished, and when the fisherman waved to them, they waved back.

But the image dissolved. His eyes looked outward and saw an ocean parched, deserted. Hot, pitiless wind threw columns of sand up at the sky. He lifted an arm to wave to no one.

The nets he tossed against the rocks on shore would catch no food. He knew this in his soul; even the tiny, dart-like lizards that his eyes showed him in the shadows were illusion, a fantasy of hunger. There was no food save the canned fruit he hid back in the cave. When those were gone, his bones would join the fishes' on the desert floor.

No one would witness his death. No one would care. He offered himself as bait, sitting in the sun. But no one came. Day after day his hopes wriggled through the coarse mesh and scurried away. Never a whisper reached his ears, but still he came each morning to show himself to the world.

A faint tremor pulsed suddenly through a line. The net slipped through the old man's hands, or perhaps it had been pulled, but still his eyes saw nothing. He told himself he had stayed too long in the sun, blinded by fire. The time had come to hide in the shade of the tree.

He tried to stand, but his legs failed, dropping him prostrate on the ground. Slowly, weakly, he crawled on his knees to the giant oak.

This tree had survived the day when fire flew down from the heavens and swatted the land with flaming wings. How the tree had stood, he did not know. The others trees had not. Their remnants lay on a plateau above the shoreline, a field of dry, blackened stumps, like headstones. Slowly the wind eroded them, devoured them. Soon the plateau would be only sand. The trees would be forgotten, like old myths. Old myths, thought the fisherman, like the son of Apollo learning to drive...

There was no life left in the tree's blackened wood, but it rose far above the sand to defiantly blot out the sun. The fisherman felt safe beneath the tree's protective shadow. It was his only friend.

Later, when the fisherman wanted to crawl back and check his lines, his legs were like bricks and would not move.

Hours passed. The sun's orb rose higher until at last it flared over the top of the tree, a bloody iris boiling in the sky. The man cowered, caught in its blind, waxy stare. He felt water drain through his skin, felt his body turn to a brittle, dry husk.

The old man closed his eyes. There was nothing left to do, nothing to see but fire. A last sigh pushed through his lips and faded. Then the wind was alone, its breath unfelt, its wails and screams unheard. The stricken wind could not grieve or shed tears, but with a passionate fierceness it buried the fisherman beneath the shifting sands.

Postscript

Haiku

Narrow confines of
tight formality leave me
unable to fin—

ABOUT THE AUTHOR

Eric Pinder was born in upstate New York, attended college in western Massachusetts, graduated, and some time later drove to northern New Hampshire in a rusty Chevy Nova packed with a few clothes, almost no furniture, and about a dozen boxes of books.

Eric's lifelong interests in science and the outdoors led to jobs at the Appalachian Mountain Club and Mount Washington Observatory. For years he lived and worked as a weather observer atop the snowy, windswept, 6288-foot summit of Mount Washington, the "Home of the World's Worst Weather." His experiences there inspired two books, *Life at the Top* and *Tying Down the Wind*. He also wrote *North to Katahdin*, a book about the appeal of mountains and wilderness.

Eric enjoys hiking and biking up the hills of New Hampshire, but has not yet qualified to join the Four Thousand Footer Club (for people who have climbed each of the state's 48 peaks rising 4000+ feet). He has, however, climbed one of those peaks (Mount Washington) at least 48 times and thinks that ought to count.

He lives in Berlin, New Hampshire.

www.ericpinder.com

I have a higher and grander standard of principle than George Washington.
He could not lie; I can, but I won't.

Mark Twain